* * * * * * *

There was nothing but darkness all around me, but I was not afraid. It was so quiet and peaceful. I felt as if I were suspended in space, free of the ground and floating in midair. But the sensation slowly began to fade away and a throbbing pain on the side of my head soon replaced it. The comfortable feeling of floating was now gone and the pain soon became so severe that I could no longer think clearly. I could not remember where I was or why I was there.

* * * * * * *

Other Large Print Editions by J.E. Terrall

Western Short Stories
  The Old West
  The Frontier
  Untamed Land
  Frontier Justice
  Tales from the Territory

Western Novels

  Conflict in Elkhorn Valley
  The Valley Ranch War

THE FRONTIER

A COLLECTION OF WESTERN SHORT STORIES

by

J.E. TERRALL

ISBN: 978-0-9994727-1-2

This is a work of fiction. Names, characters, and incidents are either a product of the author's imagination or are used fictitiously, and any resemblance to actual persons, living or dead, is purely coincidental.

Printed in the United States of America
Large print edition printed by Creatspace.com

Covers: Both front and back cover photos were taken by the author J.E. Terrall

Book Layout /
Formatting: J.E. Terrall
             Custer, South Dakota

THE FRONTIER

A COLLECTION OF WESTERN SHORT STORIES

To
Sean

THE FRONTIER

SURVIVAL

There was nothing but darkness all around me, but I was not afraid. It was so quiet and peaceful. I felt as if I was suspended in space, free of the ground and floating in midair. But the sensation slowly began to fade away and a throbbing pain on the side of my head soon replaced it. The comfortable feeling of floating was now gone and the pain soon became so severe that I could no longer think clearly. I could not remember where I was, or why I was there.

My brain slowly began to register that I was lying on the ground with my eyes closed. I was hoping the pain would go away if I laid still, but it did not. However, after some time of lying on the cool grass, I seemed to be able to tolerate the pain a little better. It was then that I felt I could slowly open my eyes.

Panic gripped me and squeezed the breath out of me. Even over the pain in my head, I could feel my heart pounding deep within my chest as I gasped for air. It slowly soaked into my consciousness that I could not see. I was blind.

I closed my eyes again in disbelief and laid back down on the cool grass. I waited for my heart rate to slow and my breathing to become steadier. I found it impossible to believe that I was blind. I was afraid to open my eyes again. But I did force myself to open them again only to discovery that I was still in total darkness, unable to see anything.

My mind filled with random thoughts and raced to remember what was around me, to remember where I was and why I was there. I closed my eyes again and listened for a noise, any noise, that might let me know I was not alone, but I could hear nothing. The silence was almost deafening and filled my mind with terror.

I tried to control my growing fears, but to little avail. It was clear to me that if I could not see and there was no one there to help me, I would not stand much of a chance of surviving for very long. I tried calling out in an effort to find someone who might be out there.

"Hello. Is anyone out there?" I shouted.

I called out several more times, but heard no response. I opened my eyes and closed them several times in the hope that I was dreaming and I would be able to see again. I saw nothing but darkness.

I don't know how long I laid on the damp grass. I told myself it was hopeless and I was going to die there in the dark, alone and helpless. Yet, something down deep within me compelled me to stay alive. I was in the middle of nowhere, all by myself. I knew my chances of surviving without sight were very slim at best. Yet a voice deep inside me told me that I had to try.

As the sudden shock of my blindness began to wear off, I tried to remember what had happened to me. What events had led up to this time? Even with the throbbing headache, I began to slowly piece together what had happened before everything went black.

Two days ago, my wife and I had left the wagon train to move north to start a ranch just north of the Platte River with her brother. We had been traveling north along a creek in a valley that was rich with thick grass when we were set upon by a small band of Indians, probably a hunting party.

During the attack, I had seen my wife, Jessie, fall with an arrow lodged deep in her chest. As I ran to her, I heard the sound of a horse running up behind me. As I turned to see where the Indian was, I felt a sharp blow on the side of my head. I could not remember anything after that.

The thought of my beloved Jessie caused tears to come to my eyes. At that point, I didn't care if I lived or died for without her I would always be alone.

I don't know how long I laid on the ground and cried for my Jessie, but I could feel myself getting cold. I realized I was also getting hungry. I had no idea how I would find food. There had been food in the wagon, but I had no idea if the wagon was still there. If it was still there, I had no idea where the wagon might be or how I would find it. After all, I couldn't see.

As I began to think about it, I began to realize I was going to have to depend on my other senses if I was to survive. I sat up and listened. The simple act of sitting up caused my head to throb even more. It took a few minutes before the pain subsided and the dizzy feeling to go away. Only then was I able to think again.

I was positive I had been left for dead, and I would be if I didn't figure out what to do. Then it occurred to me. If I had been left for dead, there was a possibility Jessie had been left for dead, too. The thought that she might still be alive gave me a small measure of renewed hope.

I rolled over and got up on my hands and knees. As I did, my head throbbed even worse. I could not let it stop me. I had to find my Jessie and take care of her.

I tried to picture the area in my mind, but had no idea as to which way was which. I could smell something burning, but I had no idea what it was. I remembered we had finished breakfast and I had just saddled my horse. I could remember I had not hitched up the wagon team, yet. I was about to do that when we were attacked.

Slowly, I crawled in the direction I thought the smell was coming from. I was very careful, as I didn't want to accidentally put my hand in a fire.

As I slowly moved across the cool damp ground, I suddenly touched something that felt different. I was sure it was a soft cotton material. I sat back on my heels and thought about it. The only thing I could think of that was made of soft cotton was Jessie's dress. I hesitated to reach out for fear that I would find her there, but I couldn't leave her lying on the cold ground, either.

Slowly, I reached out. My heart pounded in my chest so hard I thought I could hear it. My hand touched something cold, yet soft. I instantly knew I had found my Jessie. Although her skin was soft, it was cold. I did not have to see to know that she was dead.

I took her in my arms and held her to me. I don't know how long I sat there rocking back and forth as I cried for the loss of my Jessie. I did know it was cold and damp when I finally came to my senses. I had to do something. I had to care for her, but what could I do if I couldn't see?

I laid her down on the cool grass. As I sat next to her, I remembered we had a shovel tied to the side of the wagon. My immediate problem was to find the wagon. Had the Indians taken it? I was pretty sure they would take the horses, but I doubted they would take the wagon.

I reached out and patted the ground around me. There were no trees in the immediate area. I decided that if I crawled around in an effort to find the wagon, I might not be able to find my way back to my Jessie. But on the other hand, it would do me no good to drag her along with me.

With one hand touching Jessie's hand, I reached out as far as I could in the hope of finding something that would be of help. I slowly worked my way around Jessie, but found nothing but grass.

Suddenly, I felt something furry. I jerked my hand back, unsure what it might be. As soon as my heart slowed down a little, I reached out again. Once again I felt the fur. It did not move when I touched it.

I tried to think of what it might be when suddenly it came to me. It was not fur that I was feeling; it was hair, horsehair. It was one of the horses. I prayed that it was our riding horse as I had saddled it just before we were attacked. I had seen it fall just before Jessie was shot. On the saddle was a rope I could use to keep me from going too far and getting lost.

I let go of Jessie's hand and carefully worked my way around the dead animal to the saddle. I had to be careful not to lose my sense of direction. I found the rope and untied it from the saddle.

With the rope in one hand, I crawled back to Jessie. I tied one end of the rope to her wrist and the other end to my ankle. I then started crawling in the direction I thought the wagon might be located.

I can't say how long it took, but I eventually found the wagon. It had not been burned. I stood up and tied the rope to one of the wheels. I began working my way around the wagon. I soon discovered the horses used to pull the wagon were gone, but I had expected that.

As I came to the back of the wagon, I felt inside. I could not feel anything. It became clear that everything had been taken, or at least removed from the wagon. Since I could not see, I could not be sure if what had been in the wagon had been tossed out onto the ground or taken by the Indians.

By the time I found the shovel tied to the side of the wagon, I began to realize how tired and hungry I was. I wanted something to eat, but I didn't have time for that now. It would have to wait until after I cared for Jessie.

I also began to wonder what time it was. Was it night or day? I had no way of knowing, but then what difference did it make. I couldn't see anyway.

I took the shovel from the wagon and worked my way back to the where I had tied the rope. Holding onto the rope, I followed it until I came to the end. I then untied the rope from Jessie's wrist and laid her out on her back. I began digging a grave for her in the soft damp earth.

Time had no meaning with a reference to day or night. I had no idea how long I worked at the grave, but when I felt it was finished, I put the shovel on the pile of dirt that was on one side of the grave. I reached over to the other side and picked up my beloved Jessie. Carefully, I laid her in the bottom of the grave.

I wished I had a blanket to lay over her, but I didn't. As I carefully laid her out, I remembered she had been wearing an apron. I found the apron and pulled it up over her face.

I found it difficult to leave her. I held her hand for the longest time. I told her how much she meant to me and that I would miss her. I also told her that I would probably be joining her soon.

With that said, I climbed out of the grave. Being careful so I didn't accidentally fall back into the grave, I crawled around to the pile of dirt. I found the shovel and began slowly pushing the dirt in over her. At that moment, it did not matter that I could not see. My eyes were so filled with tears for my Jessie that I would not have been able to see anyway.

When I was certain that I had filled the grave, I began crawling around on my hands and knees looking for the end of my rope. When I found it, I stood up and began pulling myself back to the wagon.

The air was cool and damp causing me to remember the last few nights. They had been cool and damp, too. I assumed it was night, but I had no idea as to how late it was.

Once I got back to the wagon, I crawled inside and laid down. I was very tired, but I lay thinking about what was to become of me. I could not see, I was all alone, and I was in a strange place. I had already resigned myself to dying. I could see no way that I could survive alone, at least for very long. Gradually, sleep removed me from my present problems.

* * * *

When I finally woke and opened my eyes, I found I still could not see. I had hoped the morning would bring me sight. The one thing that was different, and that did give a small ray of hope was that my head did not seem to hurt as much.

I lay quietly trying to listen for something that would give me hope that I was not alone. The harder I tried to listen, the more I seemed to hear. Each sound brought me closer to remembering what I had seen of this place before the attack.

I could hear the sound of water running, like that of a stream or a brook. I remembered there was a stream close by. I had washed the breakfast dishes in it before I saddled the horse. I would need water if I were to survive. I could also hear the rustle of leaves and remembered the trees.

Slowly, I was able to put together a mental picture of my surroundings. As I did, I began to remember what this place had looked like before I was hit on the head. If the wagon was still facing in the same direction it had been when we were first attacked, then the stream was on the right side of the wagon and the trees were on the left.

We had been traveling along a stream through a long valley. I remembered commenting to Jessie how pretty and peaceful it was here, and that I hoped the valley where her brother had settled was as pretty.

It saddened me to think she would never see where we were planning to make our home. Tears filled my eyes as I thought of her.

Gradually, I realized I might never see it, either. Not only might I never see it, I might not survive long enough to even get there.

I began to think about my own survival. If I were to survive, I had to start thinking about what I had to do and what I would need. I could not waste my energy thinking about what might happen to me. I needed shelter and food. I needed to learn all there was to know about the small area that I was to live in. I had just a fifty-foot piece of rope that I could hang onto in order to be able to get back to the wagon. At this point my entire world was approximately a one hundred-foot diameter circle with the wagon being the center of it.

It was time to survey my little world and find out what was in it that I could use. I sat up on the end of the wagon and felt around for the end of my rope. I made certain it was still securely tied to the wagon wheel.

Checking out my world was going to take some time, but time was all I had. I needed to move slowly and cover the entire area. I decided I would gather everything I found and store it under the wagon until I could determine its value to me. In order to do this, I wanted my hands free. I tied the loose end of my rope to my belt.

I climbed down off the back of the wagon and knelt down on the ground. I began to slowly crawl, stretching my hands out in front of me and feeling around for anything I could find. I continued this for a very long time. It was a slow and tedious process, but I was able to find several things I knew had been in the wagon.

I found a blanket, one of several we had had in the wagon. I put the blanket in the back of the wagon, as I would need it before long. The other blankets must have been taken or moved outside my circle as I never found them.

I found most of our furniture, which wasn't much as we needed to travel light. There was a rocking chair, a small dresser, and a chest that had contained several of Jessie's keepsakes. So far I had not found anything I could really use, namely food. I would need food soon if I was to continue the search of my world.

As I felt around, I stumbled on a jar. I stopped and sat back on my heels as I felt the jar. I tried to remember what we had that was in jars. We had brought with us several jars of fruit Jessie had put up last fall. The thought that I had found something I could eat gave me hope.

I got a firm grip on the lid of the jar and twisted the lid until it opened. I carefully held the jar up to my face and smelled it. My heart raced with excitement when I discovered I had found a jar of peaches. I wasted no time in eating them. I didn't try to save any for later. I was too excited and too hungry to think about that. It wasn't until after I finished eating the entire contents of the jar that I realized I should have saved some for later.

Angry with myself for eating it all at once, I raised my arm to toss the jar away. Fortunately, I stopped in time. I suddenly realized I could use the jar to hold such things as water from the stream. I searched the ground around me for the lid. When I found it, I put it on the jar and carried the jar back to the wagon.

I once again began to search the grounds. Having had something to eat lifted my spirits considerably. At least now I had some small measure of hope that encouraged me to continue my search.

As I headed out from the wagon, I was sure that I was pointed in the direction of the stream. I crawled along slowly, reaching out from side to side as I searched for anything I could find. I stopped short when my hand touched something hard. Carefully, I ran my fingers over it. From the size of it, I was sure it was a box, a metal box. I could think of only two things we had that were in metal boxes. Jessie's sewing box and a box used to store crackers.

I pried open the box hoping it would be the crackers. Anything edible would be of immediate value to me as I was sure finding enough to eat was going to be my most difficult problem.

Once I managed to get the box open, I reached inside. To my disappointment, I discovered I had found Jessie's sewing box. I sat down and let out a sigh. But as I sat there, I began to realize that her sewing box could be the very thing that would save my life. In the box I would find string, needles, pins, thread and buttons. The very things I would need to made a hook and line for fishing.

With careful and painstaking effort, I crafted a hook and line for fishing by touch only. I spent the better part of my day at the stream. I don't know how long I fished, but it took me a very long time to get just one fish. The feel of that fish in my hand excited me more than almost anything in my life. In fact, that fish meant life to me.

I crawled around gathering wood for a fire. I stocked up on as much as I could find. As I searched the area for more things I could use, I found a frying pan and a pot. I also found the tin box that had the crackers inside. I gathered them close to where I had built my fire.

After my simple dinner, I could feel the air around getting cooler. I was sure it was getting dark and night would soon be upon me. I found it amazing how much better I felt and how much hope I had of surviving now that my stomach was full of crackers and fish.

I had had a very busy day and was very tired. I worried a little about my campfire being seen by Indians so I decided to let it die down and go out. I could build another one when I needed it. For tonight, I would climb into the wagon to sleep. I felt safer there and I would be up off the ground.

I lay in the wagon looking up at the sky. Although I could not see the stars, I was sure they were there. Before I fell asleep, I thought about what I would have to do tomorrow just to survive another day, but I was ready to face another day in my small world around the wagon.

* * * *

The morning sun rose with a breeze blowing. I thought I could smell rain even before I opened my eyes. I wondered what I really had for shelter. I didn't know if the wagon still had a cover over it, or if it had rags hanging on the metal hoops that normally held the cover in place.

I opened my eyes for the first time this morning. I didn't understand what was happening. I thought I could see some light, but was not really sure. My heart raced at the prospect that my eyesight might be returning. I wanted to put my hands over my eyes to see if I was really seeing some light or if it was my mind playing a terrible trick on me. I was afraid for fear I would be disappointed.

Slowly, I raised my hands up in front of my face. Nothing changed. I moved my hands closer to my face. I wasn't sure if the light was getting dimmer or if I was imagining it. But when I finally had the nerve to put my hands over my eyes and I could no longer see any light at all, I realized I was now able to see a little light. I would be able to tell if it was day or night. That was a great improvement to my morale, if nothing else.

I got out of the wagon and looked up. I was able to find a bright spot of light in the sky. I was sure it was the sun.

I sat down and felt around for one of the jars of peaches I had found and began to eat. As I sat there, I began to try to put together what had happened to me. If I could survive a few more days here, I might regain enough of my sight to be able to move on. I also understood the longer I stayed here, the greater the chance that I would be discovered by Indians. I was convinced that they were still in the area. It also meant that some wild animal looking for a meal might discover me. Not being able to see made me an easy target for an animal such as a wolf, mountain lion or bear.

Having no idea how long it might take for me to regain enough sight to see such things, I had to continue to prepare myself for the worst. I would have to continue my search for food, and something to protect myself.

I was about to get down on my hands and knees to continue the inch by inch search of my world, when it occurred to me that I had not searched the wagon very well.

I climbed back into the wagon and began to feel every inch of the inside of the wagon. As I reached under the seat, I touched something very hard and cold. I instantly knew what I had found. It was under something that might have been a piece of a trap or canvass. The Indians had apparently missed it. It was my Navy Colt.

I gripped the gun in my hand. I could feel the excitement swell in me. I now had something to protect myself with, even if I could not see what I was pointing it at. I tried to remember if it was even loaded. I thought of trying to fire off a round to find out, but didn't think that would be a good idea. For one thing, the sound would travel a long ways and might let my enemy know that I was here and still alive. For another, I would have one less shot if I needed it.

Afraid I might lose the gun if I carried it around during the search of my world, I needed to put it somewhere safe where I could get it in a hurry. Since the center of my world was the wagon, and I was tied to the wagon by a rope, I put the gun under my blanket at the very back of the wagon. It would be right next to the wheel my lifeline was tied to.

I spent the rest of the morning searching my world. I found a few more useful items and stored them under the wagon with the rest of my treasures.

As I sat fishing in the stream, I began to notice that it would get lighter, then darker, and then lighter again. I figured out that clouds drifting across the sky were occasionally blocking out the sun. I could still smell rain in the air, but I had not felt any drops of rain, yet.

When it grew darker and stayed that way, I guessed the sun had set and night had come. I made my way back to the wagon. By feeling my way around, I was able to determine that the canvass cover over the wagon was still intact. If it didn't rain too hard, or blew too much, I should be able to stay dry.

I climbed into the wagon and laid down with the blanket over me. Although I could not see, I could feel the wind gradually increase. I could also feel the temperature drop.

I could hear the canvas move in the wind. When it finally started to rain, I could hear the raindrops hitting against the canvas above me.

It wasn't long before it was raining very hard. I could see flashes of lightning through the canvas. I hoped it didn't rain too hard, as I was not sure if the canvas would protect me.

It wasn't long before I could feel the rain seep through the canvas. I wasn't certain what to do, but I thought I would be better off under the wagon. I crawled out and moved under the wagon, taking my gun with me. I leaned back against the supplies I had managed to collect as I listened to the rain.

Gradually, the rain slowed to a steady drizzle. The wind and the lightning ended. It wasn't long and I drifted off into a deep sleep.

* * * *

When morning arrived, I found myself still leaning back against my supplies. I could hear birds singing, but I was afraid to open my eyes. I wasn't positive I could take another day of blindness. I knew what little supplies I had would not last very long. I also knew I would have to move on. If I remained here very much longer, I would soon run out of wood for my fire. I also knew the Indians would most likely find me. There was no doubt in my mind what they would do to me if they found me still alive.

I could not wait any longer to find out my fate. Should I not be able to see, it might be best if I use my gun to put an end to all of this. It would certainly be quicker than starving to death or being slowly tortured and killed by Indians.

I slowly opened my eyes. My heart jumped in my chest. My breathing came almost in gasps. I realized that I could see again. It wasn't anywhere near the sight I had before I was hit on the head, but I could make out faint shadows. I could see the wagon wheel, or more accurately, I could see a shadowy outline of the wheel.

I began looking around. I found I could make out the trees, but they were not much more than fuzzy shadows. It was impossible to make out details. Everything was very blurred, but I could make out some things. The improvement in my sight lifted my spirits, to say the least.

Although I could see a little, I was still afraid to leave the wagon without taking the end of my rope with me. I was afraid if I got too far away from it, I would not be able to see to find my way back.

After putting my gun at the back of my wagon under the blanket, I walked down to the stream. When I got to the stream, the bird stopped singing. I stopped in my tracks and listened. For the longest time, I heard nothing except for the stream as it washed over the rocks. Then I began to hear the faint sound of voices. I could not make out what was being said, but I was sure it was Indians.

I don't know how long they had been watching me, but I was convinced they knew I could not see them. A cold chill ran down my spine. I had no idea how many of them were around, but I only heard two voices I could make out. I had to try to see them.

I slowly turned and carefully tried to see where they might be. Suddenly, I saw a shadow move. It had to be one of them. I didn't know what to do. I had left my gun in the wagon.

I realized it was now or never. I could stand there and let them kill me, or I could try to get back to the wagon and defend myself as much as possible. Doing nothing did not seem to be the thing for me to do. I had to make at least some show of strength.

I grabbed the rope in my hands and began pulling myself toward the wagon. I was careful not to move to fast in the hope they would not get suspicious. As I moved to the center of my world, I thought I could hear them laughing at me. I was sure they were convinced that I was totally blind. If I was correct in my thinking, it might give me just a hint of an advantage.

When I got back to the wagon, I turned my back to them. By doing that, I hoped to make them think I could not see anything.

As I stood at the back of the wagon, I slid my hand under the blanket where I had left my gun. I slowly pulled back the hammer, cocking the gun. I could feel the sweat run down my face as I listened and tried to judge just where they were. I also listened in the hope of finding out if there were more than two of them.

I could hear nothing to indicate that there were more than just the two Indians, but I could hear them moving closer to me.

They stopped laughing. Although I could not understand what they were saying, I got the impression that they were losing interest in me. I was convinced that once they lost interest in taunting me, they would simply kill me and move on.

I could feel the sweat run down the sides of my face. I nervously held the gun in my hand. If I didn't do something very soon, I was convinced they would kill me anyway. I listened and waited. I knew I would have to kill them both if I were going to survive. The fear that I might not be able to see them well enough to get them both was gradually overridden by the thought that they were going to kill me anyway.

Taking a couple of deep breaths, I gripped the gun tightly in my hands. I jerked the gun out from under the corner of my blanket and quickly swung around. I pulled the trigger as I pointed the gun at the first shadow I saw. The gun jumped in my hands at the deafening sound of it firing.

In my almost panicked state, I swung the gun at the only other shadow I could see and pulled the trigger again. Again the gun jumped in my hands. As the echo of the gunshots faded, I could hear the sound of a man cry out in pain.

I quickly pointed my gun toward the sound. I was scared to death. I could feel my whole body shake with fear. I tried not to listen to the one who was in pain, but I could not keep the sound of his cries out of my head.

I don't know how long I stood there with my gun pointed toward the sounds. I remember thinking I should finish the Indian off, but something inside me told me not to do it.

After some period of time that seemed to me to be almost forever, the cries of pain stopped. I could no longer hear anything. I thought about trying to find them and make sure they were dead, but I didn't know what I would do if they weren't. I was also afraid to try and find them in case they were not dead and were hoping I would get close enough to them so they could kill me.

I leaned back against the wagon and waited. I listened as I watched for shadows or anything that might move. It was late and the sun was just about to set when I saw a horse move out of the trees into the open. I could make out the fact it was just grazing on the long grass. Seeing the horse so relaxed and at ease, helped me feel more at ease. I had a pretty good idea that I had killed the two Indians, and that there was no one else around.

Once again I began to think more clearly. If my eyesight continued to improve, there was a chance that I might be able to get out of here. But if I were to make any real progress to get to Jessie's brother's place, I would need a horse.

I began to talk very softly to the horse. He didn't seem to mind my being there. I slowly, very slowly, moved toward him. He raised his head and backed up a step or two, but he didn't seem to object when I reached out and touched his nose.

I gave him a chance to get used to me. I was careful not to make any sudden moves.

After a while I was able to get hold of the rope the Indian had tied around his neck. I was so excited that I frightened the horse, but I managed to calm him down.

Now I had a horse. I tied the horse to the end of my rope so I would be able to find him. He didn't seem to object as he began eating the grass around the wagon.

I stayed close to the wagon that evening. I ate from the supplies I had been able to gather and then I retired to the wagon. For the first time I felt as if I might survive. I had hope. I slept well that night.

* * * *

The next morning, I opened my eyes with a degree of anticipation as well as fear. I wanted so much to be able to see well enough to be able to ride away from this place.

My heart pounded in my chest and my excitement grew beyond belief. I was able to see a little better than I had. I could make out things, although they were still very fuzzy. I could even make out the second horse that was standing just outside the circle that had become my world.

But my breath caught when I saw the two Indians that lay dead only twenty to twenty-five feet from my wagon. I climbed out of the wagon and walked toward them. The one I shot first had been shot in the center of the chest. The other poor soul had been gut shot. It had taken him some time to die.

Seeing them lying there woke me up to the fact that it might not be too long before someone missed them and came looking for them. I had to get out of there, and quickly.

I managed to get the second horse fairly easily. I packed up as much of my supplies as I could and put them on one of the horses, then saddled the other. He didn't seem to object to the saddle. It was almost as if he had had a saddle on his back before. As I was about ready to leave, I looked over at the grave of my beloved Jessie. I walked over next to it and knelt down.

"I'll be back to bring you a marker," I said softly. "I will miss you. I love you, Jessie"

I stood up and walked back to the horses. I stepped up into the saddle, then took one last look over my shoulder at the grave. After saying my last farewell, I turned back around and rode north to where her brother would be waiting for me.

THE TRAP

Four men rode into the small town of Sturgis located in the northern Black Hills in the Dakota Territory. The narrow dirt road that made up the only street in the town was little more than a two-lane cow path. The street was empty except for a horse tied out in front of the Sheriff's Office and a wagon in front of the General Store. A light gray dust swirled around the legs and feet of the horses as they plodded along the dry dusty street.

The oldest of the four riders was Frank Sparks. He had fought for the Confederate States in the War Between the States from the very beginning of the war. For the first two years of the war he had fought in the east. He was later transferred to the western front to fight along the Mississippi River.

The second rider was Sam MacGavin. He had been a member of a Confederate Cavalry unit during the Great War. He still wore his old southern army coat and a long beard that covered the scares on his face from an explosion during the war. Under his coat he wore a pair of .44 caliber Navy Colts, his gun of choice.

Sam and Frank had fought together at the battle of Vicksburg and had become friends. When the war was lost and their unit was disbanded, they drifted farther west together. First to Texas, then on north.

The short stocky rider was Jesse MacGavin, Sam's younger brother. Jesse had been too young to ride with his brother during the War Between the States, but he looked up to his big brother and wanted to be like him. Jesse had joined up with Frank and Sam a couple of years ago when the two of them decided to make their living stealing from others, especially Yankees.

The youngest rider was Billy Sparks. He was just barely seventeen. He had not fought in the Great War, but admired his brother and the stories he told about the battles that he had been in. Frank had made the war sound so exciting, almost romantic. Billy had joined the other three less than a week ago.

The riders carefully looked over each building as they moved slowly along the street toward the bank. They pulled up to the hitching rail in front of the bank and sat in their saddles as they turned and looked around.

"Kinda quiet," Billy Sparks said nervously as he looked down the deserted street.

"Yeah," Sam replied as he looked over the front of the bank.

"Too darn quiet to suit me," Frank said as he looked back over his shoulder toward the Sheriff's Office.

"Billy, take the horses. Be ready to ride," Sam said as he stepped out of the saddle and onto the ground between them.

Sam handed the reins of his horse to Billy as Frank and Jesse stepped down onto the ground. Once Billy had the reins to all the horses, Sam stepped up on the wooden walkway in front of the bank, turned and looked across the street at the Sheriff's Office. He then turned back around and looked at the front of the bank and smiled.

Sam and Jesse started into the bank while Frank looked up at Billy.

"Keep your eyes open," Frank reminded Billy, then he turned and followed Sam and Jesse into the bank.

Billy sat on his horse and looked around. He first looked one way, then the other. This was the first time for him and he was nervous. The quietness of this small town only added to his nervousness.

"Sit very still young man, and don't make a move."

The voice was coming from the corner of the bank. Although it was soft, it still had the sound of authority.

Billy had been looking over his shoulder at the Sheriff's Office. He slowly turned his head back toward the corner of the bank to see who was talking to him. His eyes got big as saucers and a cold chill ran down his spine. At first, all he could see was the edge of a wide brimmed hat sticking out from the corner of the bank. He quickly noticed the end of a double-barreled shotgun that was pointed right at him.

As Billy stared at the shotgun, a tall lean man with a long handle bar mustache slowly stepped out and away from the building. He was no more than ten feet away and the end of that shotgun looked as big as a cannon.

The man wore a bright silver star on his chest. Billy glanced back at the front of the bank for just a second. He thought about warning the others, but it was too late for that. There was no doubt in Billy's mind that this Sheriff meant business.

"Just mosey over this way nice and easy. Be very quiet and don't make any sudden moves. One wrong move, son, and you won't live to see the sun set."

Billy was confused and very scared. He looked around as if he was looking for someone to help him or at least tell him what to do.

"Make up your mind, boy," the Sheriff said softly.

Billy's gut feeling was that if he didn't do as the Sheriff said, the Sheriff would blow him right out of the saddle. That scattergun in the hands of the Sheriff was a very convincing argument for doing as he was told.

Keeping his hands in plain sight, Billy did as he was instructed. As he slowly moved around the corner of the bank, he discovered three more men. Each was well armed with a rifle or a shotgun.

Although Billy was not very smart, it was clear to him that these men had been waiting for them. Billy briefly wondered how these men knew they had come to rob their small town bank, but that thought quickly slipped away as a couple of the men grabbed him. They abruptly pulled him off his horse and took his guns.

Right now Billy had more to worry about than how the Sheriff had found out they were coming. The men who had dragged him off his horse were tying and gagging him. As soon as they were done, a couple of them led him away along with the horses.

The Sheriff raised his shotgun up in the air and moved it back and forth over his head as a signal to the men in the buildings across the street they were ready. Windows started to open, as did doors. Behind each window and door was a man with a shotgun or a rifle. The whole town was ready and waiting.

Suddenly, the front door of the bank flew open and Jesse and Frank came running out with their guns in their hands and saddlebags filled with money draped over their shoulders. They stopped short and looked around. It was obvious they had expected their horses to be waiting for them, but the horses were gone and Billy was nowhere in sight. It took them a few seconds to realize something was very wrong.

"This is Sheriff Marcus. You are surrounded. Put down your guns and put your hands up," he called out.

"It's a trap," Frank yelled as he quickly fired a shot toward the corner of the bank where Sheriff Marcus was, then turned and started to run back toward the bank door.

Jesse fired a couple of shots into the building across the street, then turned and started to follow Frank. The air was suddenly filled with the sounds of gunfire. The outlaws returned fire as best they could while scrambling for cover in the bank.

Jesse let out a scream as a bullet tore into his leg. He fell short of the door just after Frank dove inside the bank. Sam hit the bank window with his gun barrel, breaking out the glass. He tried to provide some cover fire for Frank and Jesse through the window, but it was too little too late.

Jesse was badly wounded. He tried to crawl to the door in the hope of being able to get back inside out of harms way, but it was no use. His leg had been shattered by the bullet. He reached out to Frank, his eyes pleading for Frank to reach out, take his hand and pull him into the bank.

Frank stayed behind the heavy door as he fired back at those in the building across the street. He glanced down at Jesse. He could see the pain in Jesse's face, but he could not reach him. He didn't dare try to pull Jesse inside. He would have to lean out too far. To do so would mean certain death.

Suddenly, Jesse's body jerked, and then he collapsed. There was nothing left that could be done for him now. He lay dead on the wooden walkway in front of the bank, his eyes no longer pleading for help.

Just as quickly as the shooting had started, it stopped. Inside the bank, Frank huddled down next to the door and looked out through the crack between the door and the doorframe. Sam was standing with his back to the wall next to the window. He had seen his younger brother fall, but he had been unable to do anything about it except fire back at those who had trapped them there.

"Where the hell are the horses?" Sam yelled.

"I don't know," Frank replied.

"What do we do now?" The tone of Sam's voice showed that he was scared. He knew they were trapped and he had no desire to die in this dirty little town in the middle of nowhere.

"Keep quiet. I have to think," Frank snapped back.

"They're not goin' to let us out of here alive."

Frank swung around and looked up at Sam. "I said shut up. I have to think."

Sam could see the fear and the anger in Frank's eyes. He turned away and looked back out the window. He felt sick to his stomach and there was nothing he could do about it.

"It's over. You might as well give yourselves up," a voice from the outside called out to them.

Frank looked up at Sam, then turned to look back out the door. He had immediately recognized the voice.

"Is that you Henry?" Frank called back out.

"You know it is, Frank."

"I'd heard you took up lawin', but I didn't know you was here."

"You know this Sheriff?" Sam asked as he looked down at Frank.

Frank looked up at Sam. The surprised look on Sam's face made Frank wonder what Sam was thinking.

"Yeah, I know him, but I knew him as Captain Henry Marcus. He was the Captain of my unit when I first joined the Army."

"Well, Frank?" Henry called out, the tone of his voice showing his impatience to get this over.

"I'm thinkin'."

"Ain't much to think about. We got you surrounded and we got Billy."

"You ain't hurt him any?"

"No, we ain't hurt him. But you know he will hang as soon as the judge gets here and we have us a trial. Robbin' banks is a hangin' crime around here."

"Damn," Frank said under his breath.

"What do we do, Frank. You want a make a run for it?" Sam asked.

"I don't know," Frank replied softly.

"What do you mean, you don't know?"

"Damn it, I don't know. You want to make a run for it? You go ahead. But tell me this, what are you goin' to do for a horse? They've got our horses."

Sam looked at Frank, then tipped his eyes down and looked at the floor. He knew that it was useless to just run or to try to shoot their way out.

"Say, Henry?"

"Yeah, Frank?"

"What say we make a deal?"

"It don't look to me like you got anythin' to deal with. The teller lit out the back while you was busy with us out front. But if you think you got somethin' to deal with, I'll listen. I ain't got nothin' better to do at the moment."

Frank looked around and thought for moment before he spoke. "I'll give myself up if you let Billy go."

"What?" Sam said as he looked at Frank as if he had gone crazy.

"Not much of a trade as I see it," Henry called back. "We already have Billy and you ain't going anywhere soon, except to jail or hell."

"That Henry is one tough man," Frank said as he shook his head.

"I ain't goin' to swing on the end of no rope," Sam said to Frank.

"What you plannin' on doin'? You goin' to charge them like we done them Yankees at Vicksburg?" Frank said with a note of disgust in his voice.

Sam's fear quickly turned to anger. He looked at Frank as if he wanted to kill him, but to do that would leave him alone.

Sam looked around the bank office. He wasn't sure what he was going to do. All he knew was he had to do something.

"Henry?"

"Yeah?"

"I'll give myself up if you let Billy go. You know he ain't done nothin'. He was just holdin' the horses for us."

"That makes him as guilty as you in the eyes of the law. You know that as well as I do."

Frank turned and leaned his back against the wall. He knew Henry well enough to know that he was not going to give in. Billy had set his course the day he joined up with the others and agreed to help rob the bank.

"Frank," Sam whispered.

"Yeah?"

"Take a look out there. What do you see?"

"I don't have to look. They got every man in town armed and ready to kill us if we stick our heads up."

"No. I mean look at the sky."

Frank turned his head and looked out the door at the sky. It was getting darker. Darkness meant that it would make it harder to see.

Frank turned back around and looked at Sam. A smile slowly came over his face.

"What do you think?" Sam asked as if he already knew what Frank was thinking.

"I think you're crazy as hell if you think we can make a run for it after it's dark. But you gave me an idea."

"What's that?"

"Take a look at this floor. It's made of wood."

"Yeah. So?"

"If we can pry it up and crawl under it, when they come charging in here, we could be gone."

"Yeah, but the building's surrounded. They'd catch us when we crawled out from under the building," Sam protested.

"Not if we stay under the building until tomorrow night. By then, they'd be tired of looking for us."

Sam looked at the floor, then at Frank. He wasn't sure about this idea, but he couldn't come up with a better one.

"What the hell, they goin' to hang us anyway. We might as well try it," Frank said with a grin.

"What the hell," Sam finally agreed.

"You keep watch while I try to find a good place for us to pull up some boards."

Sam nodded, then settled into watching out the window as Frank began his search for a weak place in the floor. From time to time Sam would glance over to see what Frank was doing. He thought Frank looked a little funny as he crawled around on the floor on his hands and knees looking for a place where they might be able to pull up a couple boards.

"Sam, I found a couple of loose boards over here. Give me a hand."

"Well, you guys coming out or do we have to come in and get you?" Sheriff Marcus called out.

Sam moved over next to Frank and looked at him. Together they pulled the boards up high enough they could crawl down under the building.

"Get down there and keep quiet. Don't even whisper. If we make one sound, we will hang at the end of a rope with Billy," Frank whispered. "I'll keep Henry busy while you get down there."

Frank scrambled back over next to the door.

"What's your hurry? You can't hang us until the judge gets here anyway," Frank retorted as he looked over at Sam.

Sam had three boards pulled up. It would not be easy, but they could slip through the narrow opening. Frank motioned for Sam to go ahead and crawl down under the building.

"By the way, how long before the judge will get here, Henry?" Frank asked as he watched Sam work his way under the building.

"What difference does it make?"

"I was just wonderin' how much time I'd have if I give myself up."

"You're just stallin' while you try to think of a way to escape."

"Can't fault a man for tryin', can yah?"

"Well, I've got news for you, you ain't getting' away. We got the bank surrounded and even if it gets dark, you ain't goin' to slip out of this one. I might as well tell you, the judge ain't goin' to be here for at least four days, maybe five."

"I got one more question for yah."

"What's that Frank?"

"How'd you know we was comin' here?"

"It seems like while you was plannin' on stealin' the Army payroll here, there was an Army man from Fort Meade in the room next to yours in that hotel in Spearfish. Well, he reported it to his captain, and the captain sent a messenger to let me in on it. So when you got here, we was ready for yah."

While Sheriff Marcus was talking, Frank quickly crawled across the floor and worked his way under the building. There wasn't very much room to move around under the building. It was almost impossible for them to even turn over. They would have to crawl on their bellies to move at all.

Once under the building, Frank lay flat and still. It was dark and he could just barely see his hand in front of his face. The only thing he could hear was the sound of Sam breathing, so he knew he was close. He hoped by daylight there would be enough light shining in between the cracks of the boards so they could crawl to the edge of the building. Then tomorrow night slip out from under the building and escape off into the Black Hills.

Sheriff Marcus leaned against the side of the bank. He waited for Frank to make some kind of statement, but there was nothing but silence. He had known Frank for some time. He knew him well enough to know he would not give up easily.

"Frank?" he called out, but did not get an answer.

"Frank," he called again, only louder.

Henry began to wonder what was going on in the bank. It was not like Frank not to want to talk. He knew Frank to be a man who was full of himself. At first, he thought that maybe Frank had been injured and that he might have passed out, but he didn't see Frank get hit, only Jesse.

The more he thought about it, the more he began to think that Frank was planning something. The only question was what?

Time passed slowly and Sheriff Marcus was getting a little concerned and a lot impatient. It would be dark soon. He had tried to get Frank to say something, but there was nothing but silence from the bank. Even his men were getting impatient. The standoff was getting them nowhere and it was beginning to get tiresome.

"We're going in before it gets too dark to see," Sheriff Marcus finally said.

"It could be a trap," one of his deputies reminded him.

"I know, but it's been too quiet too long. Keep me covered."

Sheriff Marcus peered around the corner of the bank and looked down the front of it. All he could see was Jesse still lying dead on the walkway.

After a brief look, he took a deep breath and then stepped out around the corner. With his gun in his hand and ready to shoot, he moved very slowly toward the door of the bank. He inched his way along until he could see just inside the door, but he could not see anything.

He again took a deep breath and moved closer to the door. When he reached the door, he knelt down and looked around the corner, but again he saw nothing. He pulled back and leaned against the wall, then motioned for others to join him at the front of the bank.

"Where are they?" his deputy whispered.

"I don't know. They might be behind the counter."

"What do we do?"

"We rush them on the count of three."

The deputy nodded that he understood and looked at the others for a sign that they were ready. As soon as they were ready, the Sheriff counted to three and they all rushed into the bank.

Much to everyone's surprise, there was no one there. They all looked at each other with dumbfounded expressions on their faces.

"Where are they?" one of the townsmen asked, looking to the Sheriff for an answer.

"Darned if I know, but they couldn't have gone far.

Sam and Frank lay still under the floor of the bank. They could hear the Sheriff and his men walking around in the bank in an effort to find where they went. It caused dust and dirt to filter down between the boards and fall on them. It was hard to breathe. Sam couldn't help himself, he coughed. It was a muffled cough, but it had been heard by Sheriff Marcus.

"Quiet everyone. I heard something," Sheriff Marcus said.

Sam and Frank could hear everything that went on above them. Now there was not a sound coming from above them.

Sweat started to run down Sam's face. His breathing became very labored and raspy. The dust and dirt filled his nose making it even harder for him to breathe. Suddenly, Sam sneezed. It was a loud sneeze that told everyone in the bank where they were.

"Come out before we start putting holes in this floor," the Sheriff called out.

When there was no response, Sheriff Marcus stepped back and fired one shot through the floor. "I said 'come out'."

Frank and Sam had trapped themselves in the narrow space under the bank. There was no escape and nothing they could do. They had put themselves in such tight quarters that they didn't even have enough room to turn over so they could at least put up a fight.

"Okay. Okay," Frank called out. "We give up."

It took a while for the Sheriff and his men to get them out from under the floorboards of the bank, but they gave up easily as they had little choice. As soon as Sheriff Marcus and his men had Sam and Frank out from under the bank, they were marched off to jail to await trial and sentencing along with Billy.

THE PURPLE GARTER SALOON

The weather was cold and damp and it had been raining most of the day. The dirt streets of the small prairie town of Plainview in the Wyoming Territory had turned to slippery mud. Winter would soon be settling in and would freeze the deep ruts in the road making them hard and bumpy. If the weather continued the way it was going, it would not be long before the rain would turn to snow and cover the town with a blanket of white.

It was a Saturday evening in early November. Most of the cattle that had been driven to town had been sold and shipped back east to the packing plants in Chicago. The ranchers in the area were beginning to settle in for the long winter and the pace of life was slowing down.

There were only about five patrons in the Purple Garter Saloon. Two of them were leaning back against the bar watching the other three at a table playing poker. The poker game had been going on for more than four hours.

Suddenly, the doors of the saloon flew open and two men in dirty clothes and mud-covered boots barged into the saloon. Everyone turned to see who they were. There were a couple of the men in the saloon that knew who they were, but chose not to say anything, at least for the time being.

The first one through the door was Gordon Hill, better know as "Boot" Hill because he had put a lot of men in the ground. Some for no other reason than they got in his way. He was short in stature, but fast and deadly with a six-gun. He was said to have a hot temper and a mean streak that was as wide as his broad shoulders.

The second one through the door was Preston O'Malley, better know as "Hard Hands" O'Malley. O'Malley had fought his way to this country from Ireland. He was fast with his fists and tough as nails, though not very smart and not very good with a gun. There were few men who could stand up to him for more than just a few minutes in a bare-knuckle, knockdown, drag-out, face to face fight.

As the two of them walked up to the bar, the two men who had been leaning against it picked up their beers and moved further down the bar, giving them plenty of room. They had no desire to tangle with the likes of these two.

"What would you like?" the barkeep asked.

"Beer," Hill replied sharply.

"Me, too," O'Malley added.

The barkeep had seen men like them before and knew enough to mind his own business. He said nothing as he poured the beer. He didn't want these two killers starting anything in his saloon.

"You seen that no-account Osborn from the Circle J around town?" Hill asked, the tone of his voice demanding an answer.

"No," the barkeep replied as he set the beers on the bar.

"You wouldn't lie to me, would you?" Hill said as he reached across the bar and grabbed the barkeep by the front of his shirt, pulling him half way across the bar.

"Say, Mister, why don't you leave him alone?" one of the men at the poker table asked.

Hill let go of the barkeep's shirt and sort of pushed him back away. He then slowly turned around to see who it was that had nerve enough to talk to him like that. His eyes looked over every one of the men at the table until his eyes came to rest on one man sitting on the far side of the table.

The man was wearing a flat brimmed hat with a silver hatband. The hat shaded his face making it hard for Hill to see his eyes. His coat was a well-tailored black frock coat. Under the coat he wore a white shirt, a black string tie and a black vest. He had the appearance of a gambler. Hill's experience with gamblers up to now had been that they were gamblers, not fighters.

O'Malley looked over the gambler then leaned close to Hill and whispered in his ear, "Careful."

Hill glanced over at his partner, then looked back at the man at the table. It was then he realized the gambler had one hand above the table and one hand below the table. The hand above the table held several playing cards, but it was the other hand that disturbed Hill. He had to wonder if the gambler had a gun in his hand. If he did, it was most likely pointed directly at him.

It angered Hill to think a tinhorn gambler had the drop on him. There was no doubt that Hill knew he was fast with a gun, but to draw when someone had the drop on you was pure suicide.

"Who are you?" Hill asked as he slowly leaned back against the bar to give the impression he was not concerned.

"Nobody you want to get to know," the gambler said, his voice showing the confidence he had in himself.

"Well, Mister "Nobody", didn't your mama teach you not to stick your nose in where it don't belong?"

"Yeah, but you're disturbing my game so that makes it my business. You blowin' off all that hot air bothers me and my friends."

The man's comment caused Hill to straighten up and start to go for his gun, but O'Malley grabbed his arm and stopped him before he could reach it. Hill looked up at his partner. There was fire in his eyes and he looked like he was ready to kill somebody and it didn't matter who.

"He'll kill you, Hill," O'Malley whispered. "This ain't the time or the place for this. He's got yah covered. Besides, we've got other things to do now. You can kill him later."

Hill continued to look at his partner for a few moments as he thought over what O'Malley had said. As his temper cooled some, he slowly turned and looked at the man at the table.

"This is your lucky day, Mister. I ain't got time to kill you now, but I'll be seeing you again. You can count on it," Hill said, his voice showing he meant what he said.

"I'm sure we'll meet again, but it may be sooner than you think," the gambler said.

Hill looked at the man as he wondered what he meant by his last comment. As Hill turned and started to walk out of the saloon, he got the feeling he should know that man. Yet to his recollection, he had never seen him before.

As the two left the saloon, everyone gave a sigh of relief. They all had been sure Hill was going to draw on the gambler.

"Say, Mister, do you know who that was you just tangled with?" the barkeep asked.

"Yeah. Why?"

"He ain't going to take it lightly that you put him down."

"Yeah, he'll probably be waiting for you when you leave," one of the men at the table added.

"Any of you know where Osborn might be found?"

"You ain't looking for him, too?" the barkeep asked.

"I might be."

"Why?" the barkeep asked.

"He's kin of mine."

The barkeep looked at the others and wondered if they were as confused as he was as to what was going on. The barkeep wondered if he should tell the gambler where Osborn was hiding.

"How do we know you're kin to Osborn?" the barkeep asked.

"His first name is Bill and he's married to my sister. My sister wrote to me and said he needed help."

"You here to help him?"

"Yeah. Any of you know why this Hill fella' wants Osborn killed?"

"It seems Bill beat Hill's little brother to death with an ax handle when he tried to force himself on Jenny, Bill's young wife," one of the men at the bar said.

"Yeah. Bill was shot and wounded by Johnny Hill in the effort to protect his wife, but he still managed to beat that bully to death," another man added.

"Bill's been in hiding ever since. He ain't in no condition to fight the likes of Hill and O'Malley," the barkeep added.

"That's why I'm here. I'm Jessup Atberry."

The name of Jessup Atberry was well known in the Wyoming Territory. He was a gambler, but he was also a well-known bounty hunter who was feared by every outlaw that had more than an ounce of sense.

"You here for the bounty on Hill and O'Malley, or to help your kin?" the barkeep asked.

"Both. The bounty will go to Bill and Jenny to help them get through the winter. He's going to have to hire some help 'til he's well enough to work again," Jessup said.

"I'll tell you where Bill is," the barkeep said. "He's in a small cabin behind the general store. Old Doc Whither has been takin' care of him."

"I'll go see him now."

"What about our game?" one of the players asked.

"It'll have to wait 'til later."

Jessup stood up and slipped his Colt back in his holster under his coat. He tipped his hat as he started toward the front door.

"Mr. Atberry, I wouldn't go out that way if I was you. Those two are likely to be waitin' on you out there in the dark. You can go out the back if you've a mind."

"Thanks."

Jessup turned around and went to the back of the saloon. He opened the door very carefully and looked out into the alley. He could not see anyone around. Jessup slipped out the door and started down the alley. He went behind the next building, then moved along side the building until he came to the front of it.

Jessup peered around the corner and looked down the street, but he didn't see anyone until he saw a match flare up at the corner of the building directly across the street from the Purple Garter Saloon. The match lit up Hill's face as he touched it to his cigarette.

It didn't take much for Jessup to understand that Hill was waiting to ambush him when he came out of the Purple Garter Saloon. The only immediate problem Jessup had was the fact he didn't know where O'Malley was hiding.

Suddenly, O'Malley appeared out of the shadows at the front of the General Store. He took a quick look around before he turned and almost ran to the corner of the building, disappearing into the darkness along side the building. It was clear that O'Malley had been hiding in the shadows ready to help Hill.

Jessup was not sure what was going on, but from the glow of Hill's cigarette it was clear the two of them were probably discussing something. There was nothing else to do but to watch and wait. Whatever O'Malley had to say to Hill must have been important for him to give away his hiding place in the shadows of the General Store. He wondered if

O'Malley might have found out where Bill was hiding.

Suddenly, Jessup saw the glow of the cigarette fall to the ground. He then heard footsteps fade away into the distance. Since the two of them did not come out of the shadows in front, they must have gone around behind the General Store. If that was the case, he could not wait to find out if they had found Bill's hiding place. He had to act and do it now.

Jessup ran across the street and around behind the building. When he got to the back corner of the building he could see O'Malley and Hill in the glow of a light coming from a window in the back of the General Store. They appeared to be sneaking up on the small cabin.

It was clear to Jessup that they had discovered Bill's hiding place and were going to kill him right there. There was no time to waste.

Jessup had to do something right now. He stepped out away from the building. He got himself set and ready to draw before he let them know he was there.

"You looking for someone," Jessup called out.

Hill swung around and took a wild shot at Jessup. The shot went wide and slammed into the corner of the building.

Jessup dove for cover behind a pile of wood, but he did not return fire. Instead he just ducked down and watched around the corner of the woodpile.

There was nothing but silence for what seemed like a very long time, although it was just a few seconds. Hill and O'Malley had ducked back in the shadows where Jessup could not see them.

"You want to get Bill, you're going to have to get me first," Jessup called out.

"With pleasure," Hill said as he fired a shot into the woodpile.

Jessup scrambled out from behind the woodpile and ducked between two buildings. Ducking behind the corner of the building, he fired a shot at Hill's feet kicking up dirt. The flying dirt made Hill dive behind some crates. O'Malley just ducked behind the small cabin.

For what seemed like an eternity there was nothing but silence. No one moved or spoke.

Hill was not sure what to do. It had been a long time since anyone had challenged him so openly. Hill was proud of the fact he was fast with a gun. He felt he had a better chance to kill this tinhorn gambler in a face to face shoot-out.

"This ain't getting us no wheres," Hill said. "You afraid to face me man to man in the street?"

"No, not as long as your friend stays out of it."

"He'll stay out if I tell him to."

"Maybe he will, maybe he won't. I don't trust you, but if your friend goes to the saloon and gives the barkeep his gun and stays there until you and I have settled this, I might be willin' to see it your way."

Again there was a long silence. Jessup thought he could hear Hill and O'Malley talking it over. He wasn't sure what would really happen, but if he could get O'Malley out of the picture it would make it a little more even.

"Okay, gambler. O'Malley will go to the saloon and give his gun to the barkeep. Then you and I can meet out in front."

"He's got to stay in the saloon until it's over between us."

"Yeah, yeah," Hill agreed impatiently.

"Okay. I want to see O'Malley leave. When the barkeep calls out and tells me that O'Malley is in the bar, you and I will start for the street."

"Okay."

Jessup watched as O'Malley stood up and came out of the shadows. He quickly moved across the alley and started between the buildings for the front of the General Store.

"You wait right there 'till the barkeep lets us know that O'Malley's in the bar," Jessup said.

"I will," Hill said.

Jessup watched and listened for any sound that would indicate that O'Malley was not going to the saloon. It seemed like it was taking forever and he was beginning to think he had made a mistake by letting O'Malley get out of the alley. He was getting nervous as he wondered if O'Malley was just taking advantage of his chance to get around behind him.

"Mr. Atberry, this is the barkeep. Mr. O'Malley is in the saloon and has given me his gun."

Jessup was not sure if this was a trick, but he had laid down the terms of the fight and he had to live by them. The barkeep didn't sound nervous or afraid. That made Jessup think that maybe, just maybe, this whole thing was going to work out.

"Okay, you heard him. Now it's your turn," Hill said with a slight chuckle in his voice. "I'll see you out front."

Jessup waited until he heard Hill move to between the buildings. He was not sure if Hill would keep his word or not. Just to be on the safe side, Jessup ran down behind the buildings so when he came out onto the street he would be a little further away from Hill. This way, Hill would not be able to ambush him when he stepped out in the street.

As he came around the corner, he could see Hill standing in the middle of the street, confident in his ability with a gun. The light from the saloon showing he was ready. He stood with his hands at his sides and his gun in his holster.

Hill was a little surprised when Jessup stepped out into the light. He was further down the street then he had expected.

"What's the matter," Hill called out. "You afraid I was goin' to ambush you?"

"I just wanted to make sure this is a fair fight."

"Gambler, what's your name. I seem to think I know you."

"The name's Jessup Atberry."

"You're no gambler. You're that bounty hunter from Cheyenne."

"Yeah."

"I thought I should know you. Well, it don't matter much to me who you are. Either way, you're a dead man."

Without another word, Hill went for his gun. His gun came up quick and the muzzle flashed as the silence of the night was filled with the sound of two shots fired at almost the same time. One bullet ripped through the well-tailored black frock coat Jessup wore and nicked the top of his gun belt at his side. The other bullet hit Gordon Hill square in the chest sending him backward onto his back in the mud.

Jessup let out a sigh of relief as he stood silently in the middle of the street. Slowly, he started moving toward Hill, never taking his eyes off him. He was sure he had hit him, but was not sure if he was dead. He walked up to Hill and saw that he was dead. He then turned and looked toward the Purple Garter Saloon. There was one more thing he had to do.

Jessup holstered his gun, then turned toward the saloon. As he stepped into the saloon, he saw O'Malley standing at the bar looking at the barkeep.

"I'll take my gun now," O'Malley said.

O'Malley had his hand out, waiting for the barkeep to give him back his gun. When the barkeep didn't give O'Malley his gun and he noticed the look on the barkeep's face, he slowly started to turn around. The smile quickly faded from his face when he saw Jessup standing just inside the door. It was clear that he had expected to see Hill.

The shocked look on O'Malley's face began to turn to anger. He didn't seem to know what to do. As rage began to replace his anger, he started across the room toward Jessup.

"Back off," Jessup said, but made no move to draw his gun or back away.

"I'll kill you with my bare hands," O'Malley said as he leaned forward and threw a hard right hook at Jessup.

Jessup was able to duck the first swing O'Malley threw at him, but the quickness of his hands caught Jessup by surprise. The second swing of O'Malley's fist caught Jessup with a glancing blow to the chin, sending Jessup staggering backward.

O'Malley was quick to follow up on his advantage. As Jessup stumbled backward, he fell over a chair. O'Malley rushed up and began kicking him in the side. Out of sheer determination, Jessup grabbed at O'Malley's legs. He managed to catch one leg and twist it, throwing O'Malley off balance.

Jessup got to his feet just as O'Malley was standing up. O'Malley quickly realized Jessup was not going to be as easy to whip as most of the men he had fought. For several minutes the two stood almost toe to toe trading punches and swinging wildly at each other.

During the melee, Jessup managed to cut O'Malley's upper lip and cause a deep bleeding cut above his eye, but not without a price. Jessup had a deep cut above one of his eyes as well as a bloody nose.

O'Malley was getting the better of the fight when he threw a left cross that caught Jessup on the side of the chin and sent him to the floor. Dazed and bleeding, Jessup tried to get up but couldn't.

O'Malley was a bit shaken by the beating he had been taking and was hesitant to move in on Jessup too quickly even when he had the advantage. That few seconds of hesitation on O'Malley's part was all Jessup needed.

He knew he could not beat O'Malley in a straight out fistfight. When O'Malley started moving in on Jessup with the intent of kicking him while he was down, Jessup waited until he was close enough, then drew his gun and laid the barrel across O'Malley's left knee.

O'Malley cried out in pain as his knee buckled and the big man dropped to the floor like a sack of flour. He grabbed his knee and rolled around on the floor in pain.

Jessup pushed himself away from O'Malley and leaned back against the wall. Holding his gun on O'Malley, he took a moment to catch his breath and try to regain enough strength to get up off the floor.

Once Jessup was finally able to get to his feet, he walked over to the bar. He leaned back against the bar so he could keep an eye on O'Malley.

"A beer, please," he said to the barkeep.

No one said a word. They all seemed to be amazed that anyone could take such a beating and still be able to stand at all. The patrons of the bar just stood around as if they were waiting for someone to tell them what to do.

Jessup took the beer, tipped it up and drank it down. He then set the glass on the bar and let out a long sigh.

"You got some place we can keep him 'til I'm ready to take him back to Cheyenne for trial?" Jessup said as he turned and looked at the barkeep.

"We got an icehouse that serves as a jail when we need it," the barkeep replied.

"Good. A couple of you guys lock him up in there 'til I'm ready to leave. You might as well put Hill in there, too."

Jessup watched as a couple of men grabbed O'Malley under the arms and dragged him out of the saloon. He then turned around and leaned up against the bar. For the first time he got a chance to see what he looked like in the mirror behind the bar. He was covered with blood and there were several cuts on his face.

"I look pretty bad, don't I," Jessup said.

"Yeah. You look like you've been in a fight," the barkeep said with a smile.

"I better clean up before I see my sister."

"You can use the room in the back."

"Thanks."

Jessup went in the back room and cleaned up as best he could under the circumstances. As soon as he was ready, he went to see his sister and her husband in the small cabin behind the General Store.

AN ANGEL ON THE PRAIRIE

Sam Yost, a guide, part time Army scout and former mountain man, was riding alone across the vast prairie of the Dakota Territory on his way from the northern Black Hills to Fort Pierre on the Missouri River. He rode along a ridge on his brown and white paint with his packhorse plodding along behind him. Sam was just minding his own business and taking in the openness of the sky and the great expanse of the prairie.

At the edge of the ridge he reined up and leaned forward to pat his horse on the neck. As he sat atop his horse, he casually looked out over the dry and barren valley below. From his vantage point on the ridge, he was surprised to see several wagons, five or six of them, in a tight circle below. It was unusual to see a wagon train this far north, especially this late in the season.

It was also strange to see a wagon train stopped and circled up in the middle of the day. It was a nice day and they should be trying to cover as much ground as possible if they planned to get to any place suitable for farming or ranching, or suitable for a winter layover.

Another thing that caused him to wonder about the wagon train was the fact there was no movement around or near the wagons. He couldn't see any horses or cattle anywhere close by, or people for that matter. It was as if the people of the wagon train had simply walked off with the livestock leaving the wagons behind. That didn't make any sense to Sam.

He thought for a moment that Indians might have attacked the wagon train and everyone had been killed and the livestock driven off. That didn't seem likely, either, as he could not see any bodies lying around. Indians were not known for burying the dead of their enemy.

He turned and reached back into his saddlebags and pulled out his field glasses. Putting them up to his eyes, he focused them on the scene below and began to scan the wagons and the area around them. He could see no movement, nor could he see any bodies lying on the ground. He could see no reason for the wagon train to have been deserted, at least from up on the ridge.

After several minutes of looking at the wagon train, he started to look up and down the valley. He could see nothing move except for a small herd of antelope that seemed to be oblivious to anything strange going on near them. Seeing the antelope grazing without a care in the world helped convince Sam the wagon train was deserted since antelope tend to stay a good distance from humans.

Giving the area one more careful look through his field glasses, he felt it was probably safe to move in a little closer. He slipped his field glasses back into his saddlebags, then selected a place where his horses could pick their way down the steep side of the ridge and into the valley below.

Being as cautious as possible and keeping a sharp eye out for trouble, he moved closer and closer to the wagons. When he was still about a hundred yards from the nearest wagon, he reined up and looked around again. There was something very unsettling about what he saw in the valley.

Carrying his rifle across his lap, he turned his horse and began moving in a wide circle around the wagons staying well clear of them. As he circled the wagons, he moved along very slowly, stopping every so often to check the ground for tracks. Between checking for tracks, he would look toward the wagons. He would also look at the area that surrounded the wagons. The last thing he wanted was to be caught in a trap.

As he moved around the outer perimeter of the wagon train, he could see between the wagons into the camp. There had been what looked like a large campfire in the center of the circle. There were no smoke or flames, and it looked as if it had burned out some time ago. He could see a coffeepot and a couple of other cooking pots had been left on the fire. It was hard to tell from a distance, but it looked as if the camp had been deserted some time ago.

After circling the entire camp, he was still as confused as ever. There were no signs of life in the camp, yet there were no signs to indicate there had been any trouble, either. There was nothing to indicate the wagon train had come under attack from Indians or anyone else. There were no arrows or bullet holes that he could see.

There were no tracks to indicate what might have happened to the animals that were sure to have been with the people of the wagon train. They would have had some oxen or mules to pull the wagons at the very least. There were also no wagon tracks to indicate which direction the wagons had come from or where they were going. It was as if the wagons had been set down from the sky right where they were. All this indicated that something such as a windstorm or thunderstorm had destroyed all the tracks. From the looks of the ground, there had been no rain in several days, yet the wagons didn't look as if they had been there very long.

"Well, boy," Sam said to his horse. "We might as well see if there's anything or anybody in the wagons."

He gave his horse a gentle nudge in the side with his heels. The horse started to move slowly toward the circle of wagons. As he moved closer, Sam drew his gun from his holster just in case it was a trap. Up until now, he had been far enough away from the wagons that he didn't think he needed to have his handgun ready to use.

Just as he was getting closer to the wagons, a shot rang out and the bullet struck the ground just in front and to the left of his horse scattering dirt in the air. The noise and the sudden shower of dirt startled his horse causing the horse to rear up and dance around nervously.

Sam dove off his horse and scrambled behind a fairly large bush. He laid low on the ground with his gun ready. He had not seen where the shot came from, but he was sure it came from one of the wagons.

It took Sam a few seconds to evaluate his situation. His horses had run off a few hundred yards, his rifle was lying in the dirt where he had dropped it, he was hiding behind a bush that provided him with very little cover, and there was nothing but wide open space between the bush and any real cover.

The suddenness of the shooting caused him to wonder what was going on and who had shot at him. More importantly, why had he been shot at?

"Hold your fire," Sam shouted.

"Stay away," a voice called back.

Sam was surprised to hear the sound of a woman's voice. He wondered if she were alone, and if so, where were the others?

"I won't hurt you. I just came down to see if there was anyone around."

"Well, now you know. It would be best if you just went on your way, Mister."

"I ain't here to hurt no one," Sam called back.

"Just stay where you are. It's for your own good."

"Yes, ma'am," Sam replied as he tipped his head down and took a deep breath.

Sam was thinking as hard as he could. Why he had not heard from a man, he wondered. Was the woman all alone? Was she the last survivor of something terrible that had happened here? And what did she mean when she said it was for his own good? There were a dozen or more questions running through his mind, but none of them would get answered if he didn't try to talk to the woman.

"Ma'am, is everything all right in there?" Sam called out.

"No," she replied.

Sam thought he could hear her voice choke a little on her reply. For the first time he could see where the woman was. He had seen a corner of the canvas top on one of the wagons move slightly and the barrel of a rifle sticking out.

"You mind telling me what the problem is. Maybe I can help."

"No one can help. It's too late," she replied.

"Ma'am, I'm going to put my gun up and come into your camp," Sam said as he slipped his pistol back into its holster.

"You can't come in here," she called back to him, her voice suddenly strong and determined.

"Why?" Sam asked as he stood up.

Her response confused him.

"There's a sickness in this camp. You must not come in for your own good."

Sam stood there for a minute looking at the wagon. He knew what some kinds of sickness could do to a wagon train like this. It would not be the first time a complete wagon train had been wiped out by a disease such as cholera or typhoid fever.

"How many are there of you?"

"Only six of us still alive, but I fear one or two of them might not last until dark."

"How many of you are there that can do anything?"

"Just myself, I'm afraid," she replied, her voice now low and hard for Sam to hear.

"How many were there when you started out?"

"There was seventy of us in thirty-one wagons when we left Omaha. But when the sickness came upon the wagon train six of the wagons with a total of seventeen people were driven off and forced to take the trail north."

"You sayin' that eleven of your people are dead?"

"Yes. And soon the rest of us will die."

Sam knew there was very little he could do to help, but he also knew he could not just ride off and leave these people to die alone in this place. He had to find some way to help them if nothing more than to keep the woman company until her time came.

"Ma'am, my name is Sam Yost. What might you be called?"

"I'm Mary, Mary Shelton."

"Mary, how are your supplies?"

"We don't have much left. I have a little water in two of the water barrels, a bit of hard tack and some jerky. I do have a bit of coffee and tea, but that's about it. I don't have any firewood left to even build a fire to heat the water," the woman said, her voice sounding very tired.

"What happened to your livestock?"

"Some were eaten and the rest just wondered off looking for grass and water."

Sam sat down on the ground with his legs crossed and tried to think of ways he could help. There had to be some way to help them, even if it was only to make dying a little easier. There had to be some way to make their last days on this earth a little more comfortable.

He mulled over in his mind what they needed the most. He came to the conclusion that she could use some fresh water, fresh meat and firewood to cook on. Since she had some water that could wait until morning.

Fresh meat she could use to make a broth to feed those who could not eat solids might help a little, but what good would the meat do them if she had no firewood to boil the water and cook the meat.

"Mary," Sam called out.

"Yes?"

"Are any of the wagons empty?"

"Yes. All of them except this one and the one to my right."

"Do you think you could strip some of the wood from the empty wagons to use to build a fire?"

"I don't know, but I could try."

"Try. When you have enough wood, you can build a fire and boil some water for tea and coffee."

"Okay, but I don't have very much water."

"There's a stream a little ways from here. I'll try to get you some more water first thing in the morning."

"How? One canteen at a time won't help much."

"If you can put a couple of empty water barrels in one of the empty wagons, I'll hook up to it with my horses and take it to the stream and get water for you."

"Isn't that risky, I mean you coming so close to us?"

"It might be, but do you have a better idea?"

"No," she admitted softly. "I really do need the water, but you shouldn't be risking your life for us."

"If you have the wagon ready, I'll get it in the morning. I'm going to leave for a little while, but I'll be back."

"Do you have to?" Mary asked.

Sam got the impression she might be worried that he would leave her and not come back. He wouldn't do that as long as there was someone alive.

"I have to go get my horses, but I'll be back soon."

Without further comment, Sam got up and walked off toward his horse. As soon as he mounted up, he rode off after his packhorse. Once he had retrieved his packhorse, he returned to where he had been sitting on the ground. He tied his horses to the large bush, unpacked his gear from his packhorse and began setting up camp for the night. He then gathered wood for a small fire for himself.

Once he had his campsite ready for the night, he went to his horse and untied him. He swung up in the saddle and looked toward the wagons. Sam turned his horse around and started down the valley toward where he had seen the antelope. As he rode away, he could hear the sound of Mary chopping wood.

By the time Sam returned to his campsite, it was starting to get dark. There were a few stars beginning to appear in the sky. The moon was still hidden behind the ridge. As he rode up to where he had left his packhorse, he noticed there was the dim glow of a fire coming from inside the circled wagons. It pleased him to know the woman had not given up.

Sam pushed the dead antelope off his saddle, got down and tied his horse. He lit his fire and began skinning the antelope. After cutting off a chunk of meat for himself, he carried the rest of the carcass as close to the wagons as he dared go.

"Mary?" he called out.

"Yes?"

"I have some fresh meat for you. I'll leave it here."

"Thank you. I'll get it as soon as you back away."

Reluctantly, Sam left the antelope carcass and retreated back to his campsite. He sat at his fire and cooked his chunk of antelope. He found himself looking toward the wagons as he ate his meal. He let out a sigh of relief when he saw the shadow of a woman between the wagons near the fire. It looked as if she was cooking the meat he had gotten for her.

It wasn't long before darkness had settled over the valley and the sky had filled with stars. Sam leaned back against his saddle and looked over at the wagons. He had not heard anything from that direction for some time. He thought that maybe Mary was trying to get a little rest, but his thoughts were interrupted when she called out to him.

"Mr. Yost?"

"Yes?"

"Thank you for staying close tonight. It was getting a bit lonely out here."

"Are you all right?"

"Yes. Mr. Cummings and his daughter passed away a little while ago."

"I'm sorry," Sam said not sure what else he could say.

"I haven't had anyone to talk to for several days now. It is good to hear a human voice again."

"Are none of the others able to talk to you?"

Mary leaned back against the side of the wagon and pulled the canvas cover back so she could see out. The glow of Sam's small fire allowed Mary to see Sam lying on his bedroll and leaning up against his saddle. This was the first rest she had gotten in two days.

"No. Jimmy Walker and his sister, Joanna, have been lying here waiting for death to come and take them. They are not in any pain at the moment, but I seriously doubt that they will live through the night."

"I'm sorry to hear that."

"Mrs. Smith is hanging on, but just barely."

"How are you doing?" Sam asked, almost afraid to ask.

Mary let out a long sigh. She was tired and had some of the symptoms of the sickness. She was still able to function fairly well, but for how long she did not know.

"I'm doing pretty well, so far."

"Do you have any signs of the sickness?"

"Yes," she replied.

Sam let out a long sigh. He knew that once the sickness was upon her, there was little that could be done. It would only be a matter of time before she would not be able to help herself.

"It's a beautiful night tonight," she said as she looked up at the sky.

"Yes, it is," Sam replied.

"I remember as a little girl lying on my back and watching the stars in the sky at my home in Ohio. Where are you from Mr. Yost?"

"No place special."

"Everyone is from some place. Where were you born?"

Sam felt she should get some rest and save her strength. But on the other hand, he liked hearing her voice.

"I was born in New York."

"Whatever brought you out here?"

"I needed room to breathe," he replied.

"I know what you mean."

"Listen, I think it would be best if you got some sleep. I'll go get water first thing in the morning."

"You're probably right, Mr. Yost. I'll have the wagon ready for you. It's the one on the far side without a canvas top. I took the canvas off it to cover the others. I also stripped as much of the wood off as I could so it would be lighter and easier for your horses to pull."

"That was very thoughtful of you. I'll say goodnight, Mary."

"Goodnight, Mr. Yost."

Sam slid down on his bedroll and closed his eyes. He couldn't get the sound of Mary's voice out of his mind. Earlier in the day she had sounded so tired and depressed, but this evening she sounded more at ease. He wished he could help her more, but to get the sickness would mean he would not be able to help at all.

Mary checked on her patients before she wrapped a blanket around herself and leaned against the side of the wagon to get a few hours of sleep. She took a moment to thank the good Lord for bringing this man to her. As she dozed off, she thought he must be some sort of angel sent to see her through her last days so she didn't have to die alone. Just having him nearby was a great comfort to her.

The next day Sam spent taking the stripped down wagon to the river. Since it was several miles to the river, it took him most of the day. It was going on evening when he returned with the wagon and its cargo of fresh water.

As he approached the other wagons, he could see a thin column of smoke rising from the center of the camp. If a fire was still going, it was a good sign. It was a sign there was still life in the camp.

Mary saw Sam coming toward the camp with the wagon. She had almost given up hope that he would return. She couldn't blame him if he had not come back, but his return gave her renewed hope. It gave her such hope that she wanted to run out and meet him, but she could not do it. She could not risk his life.

Sam moved the wagon up close to the others so Mary did not have to go so far for water. He then backed away and returned to his camp to prepare his evening meal.

The evening passed into darkness. The sky was still clear and full of stars. It was quiet and Sam began to wonder how things were going in the camp.

"Mary," he called out, but not too loudly. He didn't want to disturb her if she was sleeping.

"Yes?"

"I was just wondering if you were asleep. Are you all right?"

"Yes," she replied with a long sigh.

"What's the matter?"

"Mrs. Smith died last night and Jimmy and Joanna passed away while you were getting water."

"I'm sorry. Where are they now?"

"In a better place, I hope."

"No. I mean where are their bodies?"

"I've just wrapped them in a canvas and put them in one of the wagons with their father and Mrs. Brooks. They died yesterday evening. I'm too tired and too weak to bury them."

The mention that she was too tired to bury them worried Sam. It made him wonder if she might be getting too weak to fight the sickness.

"Did you bury all the rest of them by yourself?"

"No. I had a little help from Mr. Walker until he was too sick to help me."

"We need to do something about them before it gets hot tomorrow," Sam said.

"I know, but I just can't bury any more of them."

"I guess I'll have to do it."

"No, you can't. You'll get the sickness. Promise me that you will not come near these wagons. Just having you there to talk to has meant a lot to me."

"We can't just leave them there."

"Mr. Yost, after I'm gone I would like you to do something for me," she said, her voice creaking as she spoke.

"What is it?"

"I would like you to burn all the wagons."

"You mean burn the wagons with everyone in them?" Sam asked in surprise.

"Yes. It's the only way I can think of to stop the sickness from spreading to anyone who might come along and want to bury them after I'm gone."

As much as Sam disliked the idea of burning the wagons with the bodies in them, he knew she was right. He also knew that Mary was alone now. He would be the only one who could stop the spread of the sickness. He also knew there was nothing else he could do but wait for her time to come.

"What can I do for you now?" Sam asked after a long silence.

"Stay close by me until I'm gone, then burn all the wagons."

"I don't know," he said as he hesitated to think of what she was asking.

"Mr. Yost, you have to promise me that you will burn the wagons. You have to promise, please," she pleaded.

Sam looked down at the ground and thought about what she was asking him to do. He knew there was no choice. It had to be done.

"Mr. Yost, promise me," she insisted.

"I promise," he said reluctantly.

"Thank you. You're an angel."

"I've been called a lot of things, but that's the first time anyone called me an angel."

Sam smiled as he heard a slight chuckle come from the wagon. As far as he was concerned there had been enough talk about death and dying. He needed to hear her laugh even if it was just a little laugh.

"Mr. Yost?"

"Yes?"

"Would you mind if we talked about something else?"

"No, not at all," he replied, glad she wanted to talk about something else, too. "What would you like to talk about?"

"About you."

"Me? I'm not very interesting."

"Have you been to California?"

"Yes. Why?"

"That was where we were going. Would you tell me about it?"

"Sure. What do you want to know about it?"

"Everything. I have heard that there is an ocean there. What is the ocean like?"

"Why, Mary, it's the bluest and biggest lake you ever did see. It stretches out so far you can't see nothin' but water clear to the horizon. But it ain't water you want to drink though. It's salty and don't taste very good."

"It sounds wonderful," she said, her voice in sort of dreamy state.

"You should see the sunset in the ocean. Why it's the most beautiful thing God ever created. And the sound of the water splashing up against the shore has a rhythm like nothin' you ever heard before. It's like soft music on a quiet night.

"And them birds. I don't know what they call them, but they just seem to float in the air and swoop down and grab fish right out of the water."

"It sounds almost like heaven," Mary said as she closed her eyes and tried to envision what he was telling her.

"It's sort of like that, I guess," Sam said. "The sand on the beaches is light in color and you can see the beaches stretch out for miles up and down the coast."

Sam spent the next hour or so telling her about California. He told her about the plains, the mountains and the different flowers that dotted the land.

Mary listened, but after a while she began getting tired. She didn't want Sam to stop talking, but she was beginning to feel fatigued and needed to rest.

"Mr. Yost, do you think we could continue talking about California tomorrow? I'm kind of tired."

"Sure, Mary. You get some rest. I'll tell you more in the morning."

"Thank you. Goodnight, Mr. Yost, and thank you for staying with me. It has made this much easier for me."

"Goodnight, Mary," Sam said as he looked toward her wagon and wondered if she was feeling poorly.

Sam slid down and rested his head on his saddle. He looked up at the sky full of stars and thought there was nothing prettier in all of God's creations than a night like this one. He watched a shooting star as it sped across the sky and disappeared into the darkness. He wondered if Mary had seen the star, but was sure that she had closed her eyes to rest.

Sam lay on his bedroll and listened to the sounds of the night. It seemed to him it was quieter than usual. There were no coyotes making calls in the night. In fact there were no sounds in the night at all. It was as if everything was silently waiting for morning.

Sam woke with the sun. The air was clear and the sky was without clouds. There was no breeze to stir the dust and dirt of the dry valley floor.

Sam rose up on his elbows and looked off toward the wagons. He did not notice anything different at first, but soon realized there was no fire or smoke coming from the fire pit.

He sat up and wondered if Mary's time had come. She had seemed so happy last night to hear about California.

Sam got out his field glasses and slowly scanned the wagons. He suddenly came to a stop when he noticed a hand hanging out of the wagon where Mary had been last night. He watched the hand, but it did not move. It simply hung loose over the sideboard of the wagon. Something in Sam's head told him it was over.

"Mary," he called out, but she did not answer.

He called several more time without any kind of a response. Sam let out a sigh, then stood up. After he had his breakfast and packed his gear on his packhorse, he saddled his paint. Sam knew what he had to do. He had promised, and he would keep his promise.

He took his bandanna and put it over his nose and mouth. He then took a small can of coal oil and walked toward the wagons. The wagons were close together so he knew that once one of them was on fire the rest would catch fire.

He stood silently near the wagon where Mary had been. He made one last effort to see if she was still alive. Once he was convinced that all those in the wagons were dead, he began splashing the coal oil on the wagons.

Sam bowed his head and said a silent prayer, something he had not done for a very long time. He struck a match and tossed it in the wagon. Within a few seconds the wagon began to burn. The fire spread quickly.

Once the wagon was burning and the fire was starting to spread to the next wagon, Sam turned and walked back toward his camp. He mounted his horse and began leading his packhorse away from the burning wagons.

He slowly rode down the long narrow valley, east toward Fort Pierre. After he was well away from the burning wagons, he stopped. He turned and looked over his shoulder. It was clear that all the wagons were now fully engulfed in flames. With sadness in his heart, he turned and rode on. He had done what he could, and he had done what he had promised.

The thought passed through his mind that if he was an angel as Mary had said, he must be the angel of death. The angel that would make sure all those poor souls would get to that better place Mary had mentioned.

THE TRAPPER

It was the beginning of the summer of 1843 in the Dakota Territory. A white man was carefully stacking bundles of beaver pelts and fox furs in a large birch bark canoe on the bank of the Elk River. The man was dressed in buckskins and a beaver hat. A long sharp knife dangled at his side. He had a flintlock pistol tucked in his belt while his Hawkins musket was only a few feet away leaning against the bow of the canoe.

Out of the bushes came an Indian woman carrying another bundle of pelts. She was wearing a buckskin skirt and a jacket covered with beads and a few small feathers. At her hip she carried a long sharp knife, just like the man's.

After the woman dropped the bundle near the canoe, she reached up and wiped the sweat from her brow. She put her hands on the small of her back and arched her back in an effort to take the soreness out of it as she watched her man load the furs into the canoe.

"How long will you be gone?" the woman asked in Lakota, the native language of her people, the Sioux.

"I will be gone for about two moons," the man replied in her language.

"It will be a long time."

"You will have plenty to do while I am away. Since furs are getting harder to come by, you will need to tend to the garden and care for the animals until I return. Your brother told me that he will help you and watch over you until I return."

"Hurry back. I will miss you."

"I will miss you, too."

Samuel Hicks finished securing the pelts in the canoe and loaded his supplies for the trip. As soon as he was ready, he took a few minutes to kiss his wife goodbye before he pushed off from the shore and started down the river.

As he started around a bend in the river, he looked back. His wife was still standing on the bank. He waved to her and she waved back. She was soon out of sight and he suddenly felt very much alone.

The water was high with the spring runoff from the mountains and the recent rains. He moved along at a smooth, steady pace. This past winter had been fairly mild, making for very good trapping, but he knew that it would not be long before the trapping would not provide for him and his family. When he returned, he would change his ways and become a rancher. The money from the furs would help him get started as a rancher.

If the start of his trip to Fort Pierre was any indication of how it was going to be, it could prove to be an uneventful trip. The weather had been good with only an occasional afternoon thunderstorm. During periods of light rain, Sam would continue on his journey. Only when it would rain hard did he seek shelter along the bank of the river in among the large cottonwood trees. Within a few days, Sam had gone from the Elk River into the Cheyenne River that would take him to the Missouri River above Fort Pierre.

It was late one afternoon when Sam noticed three riders off in the distance. They seemed to be riding in the same direction he was traveling. As the day went on, the riders continued to stay even with him. They were too far away for him to tell who they were, but their presence troubled him. It would not be the first time that a trapper had been robbed of his furs on his way to market.

As the afternoon passed into evening, Sam started watching the other side of the river for anyone who might be trailing him. He didn't see anyone, but the riders he had seen earlier were still there. They were still staying well away from the riverbank, far enough away so that he would not be able to identify them later, but close enough to keep an eye on him.

It was getting dark and Sam needed to make camp soon. He turned away from the bank and headed across the river to the far side. He did not think the riders would cross the river because it was wide and deep in this area.

As Sam reached the far side of the river, he ran the bow of his canoe up on the sandy bank. He quickly got out and pulled the canoe up on the bank so it could not float away. He immediately began to set up camp near his canoe while still keeping a wary eye on the other side of the river. He built a small fire and laid out his bedroll.

Every once in a while Sam would glance across the river to see where the riders were. As he cooked his dinner over his fire, he saw the riders setting up camp directly across the river from him.

Sam did not like having these men so close to him. It made him nervous. He was convinced they were trailing him for the sole purpose of stealing his furs, but they seemed to be in no hurry to do so.

As darkness covered the land, Sam decided to let his fire go out. He would wait a little while, and then he would quietly put his canoe back in the water and silently slip away in the night. With the river so wide, he was sure he could navigate his way down the river without difficulty, putting several miles between them by morning.

Sam waited patiently for the small half moon to go behind a cloud. When it did, he quickly gathered his bedroll and took it silently to his canoe. The only sound was that of the ripples of the river gently splashing against a log at the edge of the shore and the canoe.

He was just beginning to push his canoe off the sandy bank when the thought he heard something behind him. As he turned around, he got just a split second glance of the figure of a man before he felt a sudden pain on the side of his head and everything went black.

* * * *

It was still dark when Sam opened his eyes. His head throbbed with pain. As the fog cleared from his head, he sat up to look around. The throbbing of his head caused him to close his eyes again and wait for it to subside a little. When the pain became tolerable, he opened his eyes and saw his canoe with all his furs and supplies was gone.

He instinctively looked across the river to where the riders had set up camp. He could not see anything. There was no sign of a fire or anything else.

Sam crawled down to the edge of the river and splashed some cool water on his face. It seemed to help relieve some of the pain and allowed him to think more clearly. He sat down on the bank and looked across the river.

Thinking back over the day, Sam was sure the riders on the other side of the river had wanted him to see them. They kept him distracted from the one on his side of the river, the one that presented the greatest danger to him. It angered him to think he had fallen for such an old trick.

Slowly, Sam closed his eyes and tried to remember what he had seen just before everything went blank. It had been dark when he had been attacked, but Sam knew if he concentrated he might remember something that would make it possible for him to identify his attacker if he found him.

A picture slowly started to form in his mind. The man who attacked him was about five foot five inches tall and was most likely a half-breed. He had sharp features and a long scare on his left cheek that ran from just below his eye and down his cheek to a point even with his mouth.

Sam tried to remember if he had ever seen such a man before, but nothing came to mind. Sam knew he had to go after the men and get his furs back or die trying. He knew the only place within five hundred miles where anyone could sell furs was at Fort Pierre. Sam was sure those who took his furs would want to sell them as soon as possible and get away.

Sam stood up, took a quick look around. The small pouch that he carried some hard tack biscuits and a few pieces of jerky in was lying next to where his canoe had been. He quickly picked it up and swung the strap over his shoulder. He then set out to catch up with the men who had taken his furs.

He began his quest to catch up with them by walking, gradually increasing his pace as his head began to feel better. It wasn't long before he was jogging along the bank of the river, covering a lot of ground with a steady pace.

As the sun began to come up, he kept a close watch for the riders and his canoe. He was sure they would have either sunk his canoe, or they would have simply let his canoe float down the river after loading the furs on their horses. Either way, he was on foot and would have to move quickly if he was to catch them.

It was about noon when he spotted his canoe. It was half under water and tangled up in an old cottonwood that had fallen into the river. With the canoe, he could make better time.

Sam waded out into the water to retrieve his canoe, hoping that it was not damaged. The water was waist deep and with the current it was difficult for him to pull the canoe from the tangle of branches. Once he got the canoe loose, he dragged it up on the sandy bank. As he tipped it over to empty the water out of it, he could not help but smile at his good fortune. Not only was the canoe undamaged, but his spare canoe paddle was still inside it.

Sam immediately tipped the canoe right side up and pushed it back into the river. Grabbing his paddle, he began paddling on down the river. He had no idea how far the thieves were ahead of him, but he now had a chance to catch up with them.

Sam kept the canoe moving down the river. It was well past noon before he turned the canoe toward the bank. He was beginning to feel the strain of pushing so hard.

Once on shore, he pulled the canoe up onto the bank and stretched his tired muscles. Even his legs were getting stiff. He walked a short way away from the riverbank in order to loosen up his stiff muscles. As he did, he studied the ground for some sign that he was right in choosing the direction the thieves had taken.

Just as he was about to turn around and return to the canoe, he noticed tracks in a small area of soft dirt. The tracks were those of four horses and four men. There had been three men on one side of the river, plus the one that attacked him. The tracks were fresh. If they each had a horse that would account for the horses. The fact that the men were walking indicated to Sam they had put his furs on the horses and were leading them.

Since the tracks were fairly fresh, Sam was certain he was gaining on them. If all went well, he might be able to catch up with them before they got to Fort Pierre. The thought that he might actually catch them gave him renewed energy.

Sam almost ran back to his canoe. He quickly pushed off and began moving down the river again, only this time he stayed close to the bank. He wanted to be ready to beach his canoe very quickly if he should spot them.

The afternoon turned into evening and the sun was beginning to set. Sam wasn't sure how much longer he could continue. He certainly didn't want to go past them in the dark of night. Besides, he was getting very hungry. He had not taken the time to eat. He had just had a few handfuls of water from the river to drink as he paddled down the river.

As he was about to turn his canoe toward the bank and stop for the night, he noticed a flickering light up ahead. He was sure it was a campfire. His enemies would not be expecting him as they had taken his canoe and left him on foot.

He quickly turned the bow of his canoe into the bank. When it rode up on the bank, he quickly jumped out and pulled it up on the bank. Since the canoe was empty, it was light enough that he could pick it up. He moved it into some high brush behind a fallen cottonwood tree.

He moved back to the bank of the river where he could see the campfire and sat down behind a rock. He ate some of his hard tack and jerky and drank some water from the river. Having something in his stomach made him feel better. The one thing he hadn't done was figure out how he was going to get his furs back.

After putting what little food he had left back in his pouch, he carefully hid it behind some brush. He then started working his way toward the campfire. Since he didn't want them to find his canoe, he made a wide circle around their camp so he could approach it from the other side. As he did, he would stop every so often and look in on them. The one thing he noticed was there were only three of them sleeping near the fire. There was the one who had attacked him and two others. The fourth member of the band of thieves was not there.

Sam was sure he was back in the darkness away from the fire. He was most likely taking his turn as guard. It was kind of unnerving for Sam not knowing where the fourth man was.

Suddenly, he heard the snapping of a twig near the river. Someone was moving around. Sam slipped back further into the darkness, moving with great care.

When he didn't see the forth man appear near the fire, he slowly and quietly started to move around toward where he had heard the noise. Much to his surprise, he found the fourth man sitting on a log just looking out over the river. Sam wondered if they might be a little worried that he would come down the river after them.

Sam was not sure just what to do at this point. He wanted to kill this man if for no other reason than to reduce their numbers. But to do that would bring attention to himself and they would be more alert and ready when he tried to recover his furs.

There was an unexpected noise from some critter in the brush behind Sam. The noise caused Sam to turn around and look. The man sitting on the log must have heard the noise as well. The man stood up and pointed his gun toward Sam.

"Who's there?" the young man called out, his voice showing how nervous he was.

Then without any warning, he fired a shot that hit a branch beside Sam's head. The shot was too close for comfort. Sam jumped to his feet and rushed the man before he could reload his musket.

Sam tackled the young man and hit him on the head with a heavy stick he picked up from the ground, knocking the young man out. Sam was still well aware that the others would have heard the shot and would be coming to his aid. He then grabbed the young man's powder horn and bag and his musket and ran off into the woods. He quickly ducked down behind some bushes to hide.

Sam could hear the commotion going on where he left the young man. Everyone was wondering what had happened to him. They all seemed to think it was someone other than Sam who was trying to steal the furs, except for the half-breed. He was the only one who was convinced that Sam could have caught up with them and was trying to get his furs back.

"Did you see who hit you," one voice asked.

"No. All I saw was something jump out at me from where I shot. I couldn't say who it was."

"Was it the trapper," the half-breed asked.

"I don't think so. This guy was much bigger. I think it was an Indian."

"An Indian?" the half-breed asked.

"Yeah," the young man replied as he felt the bump on the side of his head.

"What makes you think he was an Indian?"

"He moved like one, you know, quiet and quick."

"Okay, enough," the large man with a red beard said. "We don't have time for guessing. Johnny, you get some rest. Pierre, you take watch."

"Oui," Pierre replied.

"You think he will come back," Johnny asked.

"Not tonight," the big man replied.

Sam stayed hidden in the bush and listened. He had a pretty good idea who the Frenchman was. It was Pierre L'avoue. He had been a trapper for many years, but turned to stealing furs when trapping became too much work for him.

The red bearded man was Louis Greene. He was not well known in these parts, but he had a reputation of being mean and nasty. It was said that he would do almost anything for money including killing for it.

Sam didn't know who the young man was, but from what was said and the way he was treated it was pretty clear he was related to Greene in some way. He might have been a nephew or younger brother.

There was no doubt in Sam's mind who the half-breed was. He had lived with the Sioux a number of years ago, but left shortly after he had a fight with the Chief's son that caused a riff in his relationship with the Chief. His name was Black Lion, Gerald Black Lion.

After the camp seemed to settle down, Sam quietly moved back around to his canoe. He then pushed it out into the river and in the dark of night slipped on down stream to where he could wait for them. And while he was waiting, he could figure out how he would get his furs back.

The only way he was going to get his furs back was to steal them back. He knew it would not be easy as he was outnumbered four to one. The more he thought about it, the more he realized he would have no choice but to kill them. It was a hard land without any laws to protect the rights of the individual. Out here he had to protect his own rights and dispense his own justice any way he could.

Sam found a place along the edge of the river where he could ambush them. It seemed to be the coward's way of doing it, but what choice did he have? If he could disable a couple of them, he might be able to get his belongings back.

That night Sam slept restlessly. He had positioned himself in a place where he had a good view of the trail running along the river. It was not a very large area and he would have to shoot straight and true if he were to disable them. It was now time to simply wait and be ready.

The sun came up slowly and the ground was covered with a mist that gave everything a ghostly appearance. It would make it more difficult to select his target, but it would give him good cover to escape. His tactic was simple, hit and run until all of them were disabled or dead.

Sam could hear the four riders before he actually saw them, and what he saw were just shadowy images of them in the mist. He wanted to get the half-breed first. Sam felt he was the most dangerous. Then if possible, he would try to kill Louis Greene.

He took careful aim at the image he thought was the half-breed. Since they were walking almost side by side, he had a hard time distinguishing who was who. He slowly pulled back the trigger on the musket. There was a flash and a loud bang as the musket fired. There was a cry of pain, but he didn't have time to look and see who he had hit. He needed to get his musket reloaded.

As he reloaded the musket, he would glance up to see if they might attack him. He could see no movement for the longest time. All he could see were the horses with their packs of his furs. All he could hear were the cries of pain coming from one of them. He waited and listened.

He looked up at the sky. The sun was growing hotter and it would not be long before it would burn the mist off the ground. He needed to be gone before that happened, before his hiding place could be seen.

Just then, he saw some movement. It was one of them trying to get a better position. Sam took careful aim and pulled the trigger. The gun jumped in his hands, but his aim was true. He saw the figure fall over backward.

He had hit another one of them, but he did not cry out in pain.

Sam didn't wait to reload this time. The mist was starting to clear. If he was to get away, he had to move fast and he had to move now. He ran to the river, jumped in his canoe and raced on down the river as fast as he could.

There was one other place along the trail to Fort Pierre where they would have to come close to the river before the trail turned away from the river. With what had just happened, they might be expecting him to be waiting for them there.

After that, the trail went inland about a mile or more. It would be some fifteen miles before it meandered back toward the river. It was only five miles to Fort Pierre after the trail rejoined the river. It gave Sam little time to get his furs back. Once they got to Fort Pierre, they could sell his furs and he would not be able to prove they were stolen from him.

Sam decided he would surprise them. He landed his canoe close to where the trail turned inland. He hid it in the heavy brush along the edge of the river before moving along the trail away from the river. When he got far enough from the river where they might not expect him, he settled in to wait. From his hiding place he would be able to see them coming while they were still a long way away.

Time passed slowly as he waited. It seemed to take forever before they came around a corner of the trail where he could see them. He had not known just how much his first attack on them had hurt them until now. There were only three of them now and one was limping along. It was clear he had hurt one pretty badly, and had most likely killed one. The one that was missing was the half-breed. He must have been the one he had killed.

As the thieves came out into a clearing right under the ledge Sam had selected for his hiding place, they stopped. Sam could see that the one limping was the young man. Even from a distance, Sam could see his side was covered with blood. He was bleeding quite badly.

"I can't go any further," the young man said as he stopped.

He was having trouble just standing. His body swayed, and then he fell over face down.

"Leave him," Pierre said as Louis Greene started to move toward the young man.

"I won't leave him. He is going to Fort Pierre with us," Greene insisted.

"He will just slow us down. Besides, he is dead anyway. I will not wait," Pierre said angrily.

"You will wait, or I'll kill you right here," Greene said as he drew his pistol from his wide belt and pointed it at Pierre.

"You are crazy. This will not help him."

"Maybe it won't, but you ain't getting his share of the furs," Greene said.

"Okay. We will put him on a horse."

Sam watched as the two men lifted the young man and laid him over one of the horses on top of the furs. After they tied him on the horse, Greene took up the reins of his horse and one other.

"Let's go."

"Oui. Let us go, then," Pierre said.

Sam watched as they started to move closer to him. He now had only two men to deal with. It was time to take his furs back.

"Stop right there," Sam called out.

They stopped and looked around. They could not see Sam as he was well hidden in the rocks.

"What do you want," Pierre called out.

"I want my furs."

"Ahh, so it is you that has been giving us trouble."

"Yes, and if you don't want any more you will put down your guns and walk back up the trail where I can keep an eye on you."

"But suppose we don't want to put down our guns," Greene said. "There are two of us and only one of you."

"If you don't put your guns down, there will be only one of you. The only question is which one?"

"You would shoot one of us in cold blood?" Pierre asked.

"I would give you the same chance the half-breed gave me. None."

Sam noticed that as they talked, Louis Greene slowly moved closer to the horses. He was planning on using the horses as cover. Sam carefully sighted his rifle directly at Greene and pulled back the hammer.

"One more move, Greene, and you're dead."

Greene froze in his tracks. Sam wasn't sure just what he had gotten himself into. The one thing he was sure of was he had not planned this out very well. He had one gun, the rifle he had taken off the young man, which could only fire once before it had to be reloaded. On the other hand, they each had a rifle and a pistol. Even if he did kill Greene, Pierre had time to shoot at him at least a couple of times. Also, if he fired at them, his position in the rocks would be exposed to them.

Greene looked at Pierre. They could not stand there all day and do nothing. It was time to make a move.

"When I jump for the ditch, you dive into those bushes over there," Greene said in a whisper.

Pierre glanced at the bushes where he was to go. He didn't like the small amount of cover they provided, but he didn't see as there was much they could do. He turned back and nodded slightly that he understood.

Greene looked back up at the rocks in an effort to see where Sam was hidden, but he could not see him. Their only chance was to duck for cover.

Suddenly, Greene started to move toward a ditch. There was the sound of a rifle shot from the rocks above him. The bullet caught Greene in the knee causing him to fall before he made it to the ditch.

"Damn," Greene screamed in pain as he doubled up on the edge of the trail.

Sam quickly pulled back from the edge and began reloading his rifle. As he did, there were two shots fired in his direction. One of them ricocheted off the rocks above his head dropping small pieces of rock and dirt on him.

The shooting stopped as quickly as it began. Sam had reloaded his rifle. He carefully looked over the rocks at the scene below. The four horses had run back up the trail a little ways and seemed confused. Greene laid curled up on the trail holding his knee. The Frenchman, Pierre, was nowhere in sight.

Greene was out of the fight, but Pierre was still out there somewhere. He was probably waiting for Sam to show himself.

Sam showed as little of himself as he could. He didn't want to give Pierre anything to shoot at, but he had to find him. Looking out over the area, he looked for anything that might give Pierre's position away. There was nothing moving, not even a breeze.

It was the lack of a breeze that gave Pierre away. Sam noticed a slight movement in the tall grass on the far side of the trail. The slight wave in the grass seemed to be moving toward a line of trees. If it was Pierre moving in the grass, Sam could not let him get to the trees. From the trees, Pierre would have good cover and would be able to see where Sam was hiding.

Sam laid his rifle over the large rock that protected him and took careful aim at the waving grass. Holding his sights on the waving grass as it moved closer and closer to the trees.

Although Sam could not see Pierre, he was sure he was making the grass move. He had to make a decision. If he shot at the moving grass and missed Pierre, Pierre could easily get up and run for cover before he could reload and fire again. If it wasn't Pierre making the grass move, he would open himself to being fired upon from some place else. Either way, he was taking a chance. And either way, he couldn't let Pierre get into the trees.

Sam took aim at the waving grass and slowly pulled the trigger. The rifle fired its lead ball into the grass. There was a sudden cry of pain as Pierre rose up and fell over. Sam had hit his mark, but as soon as Pierre disappeared back in the tall grass it became a game of wills.

Sam looked at the scene below. He now had one man wounded and lying in the road where he could see him. He had another lying in the tall grass, but he could not be seen. That made him very dangerous.

"You ready to give up, Pierre?"

"I'm hurt. I'm bleeding."

"You asked for it when you took my pelts," Sam said.

"Help me," he called out.

"Not until you toss your guns out on the trail."

There was silence for a long time before Sam saw a rifle appear above the grass. He watched it as it flew through the air and landed just short of the trail.

"Your pistol, too."

A pistol followed shortly. It landed in the middle of the trail.

Sam looked around. He still didn't have Greene's guns, but he could see that Greene would not be able to reach them from where he lay.

Sam started to climb down from the rocks onto the trail. He slowly moved along the trail toward Greene, while keeping an eye on the grass where Pierre lay. His rifle was ready just in case either of them had any fight left in them.

Since Greene was the easiest one to see, Sam pointed his gun toward the grass and started into the grass to retrieve Pierre. Just as he came upon Pierre, Pierre jumped up and slashed at Sam with his knife. Sam stumbled backwards to avoid the sharp blade of the knife. As he did, he stumbled and his gun when off. The shot hit Pierre square in the chest, killing him instantly.

Sam sat on the ground and looked at the Frenchman. The front of his shirt was soaked with blood. Pierre's plan had failed, and had cost him his life.

After taking a deep breath, Sam got up. He walked back toward Greene. As he came to Greene's rifle and pistol, he picked them up.

"Help me," Greene pleaded.

"Why? Why should I help you?"

"I'm in pain. I can't walk."

"Maybe I should leave you here to die. I doubt there will be anyone along this trail for days, maybe not even for weeks."

"Don't leave me," he pleaded again.

Sam ignored him as he walked past him and started down the trail to where the horses were now grazing. He tied one to another then took the lead horse and started back along the trail. When he got close to Greene he untied the young man and pulled him off the horse. He laid him along the side of the trail only a few feet from Greene.

Sam picked up the reins of the lead horse and began walking down the trail toward Fort

Pierre. He walked right past Louis Greene without so much as giving him a glance. Sam knew it was not right to leave him there to die. He knew Greene would have shot him without a second thought and left him to die.

After going down the trail for a little ways, Sam stopped and turned around. He looked at the big man laying on the trail. He was a pitiful sight. He was also a pitiful excuse for a man, but he was a man none the less.

Sam tied the reins of the lead horse to a nearby tree then took a canteen off the pack. He walked up to Greene and looked down at him. He reached out and handed him the canteen of water.

"I will send someone back for you," Sam said. "If I ever see you again, I will not hesitate to kill you on the spot."

Greene looked up at Sam. Slowly, he reached out and took the canteen. He knew Sam had done more for him than he would have done if the roles were reversed.

Sam then turned around and walked away. He took the horses and continued on his way to Fort Pierre where he sold his furs. He returned to his wife with the horses he had taken from the thieves. Upon his return, he and his wife started ranching at the foot of the Black Hills.

THE TEXAS JAILHOUSE

A small stone building set back away from a long narrow dirt road somewhere in southwestern Texas. The reddish stone slowly baked in the hot Texas sun while a lone man sat on a wooden bench out in front. A dull silver badge rested on the man's sweat-soaked shirt just above the left breast pocket as he leaned back against the building. He had his hat pulled down to protect his eyes from the glaring sun.

Inside the building were two men. They sat on narrow cots inside cages that were only four feet wide, five feet tall and six feet long. The cages were made of steel bands riveted together to make the jail cells. The heavy steel cages had large steel hinges on the doors and big locks held them securely closed.

The stone building had only three windows with iron bars over each of them. There was no breeze coming through the windows making the inside of the jail hot and miserable for the two prisoners locked inside.

"Hey! Can we get some water?" one of the men yelled from inside.

The deputy sitting out front did not answer. He simply turned his head slightly and looked toward the door of the small Texas jailhouse. It was hot for him, too. There were no nearby trees to provide shade from the blazing sun, and there was no breeze to cool him, either. It was a good hundred yards across the courtyard to the nearest pump for water.

"Hey! You gone deaf out there?"

"Hold your horses," the deputy called back.

The deputy let out a long sigh and then raised himself up off the bench. It was almost too hot to even move. He reached inside the door of the jailhouse and picked up a bucket. He started across the courtyard toward the only house within miles. It had a pump located in the front yard. He put the bucket under the spout and began pumping the long handle up and down. It took four or five pumps of the handle before the life-giving water began to flow out.

Suddenly there were the sounds of gunshots coming from the jail. The deputy stopped pumping and looked across the courtyard toward the jailhouse. For a moment he saw nothing, but then he saw his two prisoners come running out of the jailhouse, one of them holding his arm as if it were injured.

Realizing what was happening, he started to draw his gun. Before he had cleared leather, two riders leading two extra horses came charging out of a ravine behind the jailhouse. The deputy began firing his gun at the men, but he was too late. A bullet ripped through his side spinning him around and knocking him to the ground.

As he lay on the ground, he could see his prisoners run for the horses. They jumped in the saddles and rode off as fast as they could. He tried to get up, but the pain in his side was too much for him. He knew he was in no condition to go after them. All he could do was lay there and watch them ride off across the flat, dry land.

He did not recognize the two who had helped his prisoners escape, but it didn't matter. He knew that without immediate help, he would not last long enough to tell anyone who they were, anyway.

It was well past noon and the sun was beginning to move across the sky to the west when Sheriff Sam Stillman returned to his home from a trip to the rail siding to telegraph for a judge. As he rode up, he saw his deputy lying on the ground near the well. Even from a distance he could see he was dead. The dark color of the deputy's shirt was all he needed to see to know what had happened.

Sheriff Stillman had been a lawman for many years. He was a hard man with hard principles, and the determination and skill to carry out what he knew had to be done. He would first take care of his deputy and friend, and then he would go after the men who had killed him.

After Sheriff Stillman had buried his friend, he filled several canteens with water. He packed his packhorse with supplies and put his rifle on his saddle. As soon as he was ready, he mounted up and started off in the direction the prisoners had gone. He set a pace that was easy on his horses, yet would cover ground fairly fast.

There were no illusions in the mind of Sheriff Stillman. He knew what it was like in this part of Texas at this time of year. Following these men would be like following them into Hell. The heat was well over a hundred degrees during the day and water holes were few and far between, especially if you didn't know where to look for them.

It would soon be dark, but there would be a full moon. Stillman had some idea of how much of a head start the outlaws had. He had taken the time to look over their tracks. Four men with four horses, and all of them on the run. Without very much for supplies, they would not be able to get very far. From the direction they were traveling, it was unlikely they knew the country very well. It was clear that they were headed to Mexico, but they had picked the hard way to get there.

He also could tell by their tracks they were traveling hard and fast. That would mean their horses would suffer. If they pushed the horses too hard, they could kill them and end up on foot. Being on foot was not a pleasant thought out here.

Stillman rode well into the night before he stopped to rest. He knew that it was best for him to travel as much at night as possible. It would not only be easier on him, but it would be easier on his animals.

After he took care of his horses, he bedded down for the rest of the night. He did not build a fire as the glow of a fire could be seen for miles in the vast open land. He did not want his fugitives knowing where he was and that he was on their trail.

Stillman was up and ready to move on before the sun was above the distant hills. He again checked their tracks before he started out. From the looks of the tracks, at least one of the horses was going lame. If they turned the horse loose that would mean two would have to ride one horse, and that would slow them down even more.

The sun was high in the hot Texas sky when Stillman noticed something up ahead. He reined up and reached into his saddlebags for his field glasses. He knew he was gaining ground on the men who had killed his deputy, but he had not expected to catch up with them so soon.

Standing with its head hung down was one of the horses he had been tracking. It was clear it was the one that had gone lame as it hobbled when it tried to move closer to a small amount of shade provided by a desert bush.

He took a minute to scan the horizon in the hope of finding the fugitives, but he saw nothing. After slipping his field glasses back in his saddlebags, he nudged his horses on. It wasn't long before he came close to the lame horse. It was obvious the horse was suffering from the pain of his right foreleg and from a lack of water. Stillman would have liked to help the poor animal, but to do so might leave him short of supplies. To try to take the animal with him would simply slow him down, and to shoot the animal to end its suffering might be heard by the fugitives.

As Stillman rode past the animal, it tried to follow. The horse was unable to keep up and was soon left far behind.

Stillman continued to move at a steady pace across the dry land. The tracks he followed showed that one of the men was doing a lot of walking. The men he was after were hard, mean and unforgiving. He figured the fugitive that was walking was forced to do so because his horse pulled up lame and had to be left behind.

It was late in the afternoon when Stillman found a place in the dirt where someone had fallen. As he looked off across the wide-open land, he began to think it would not be long before he would catch up with at least one of them. Since he knew the kind of men he was trailing, he knew anyone who could not keep up on his own would be left behind just like the horse had been. These men were ruthless.

After giving his horses a drink of water from his hat, he mounted up and nudged them on. The tracks that he followed now were indicating that the fugitives were slowing down. If he could press on into the night, he might be almost upon them by early the next day.

Sheriff Stillman walked his horses as he carefully watched for tracks. He continued on until it was too dark to see their tracks any more. Since he didn't want to lose their tracks, he stopped and tied his horses. After he fed and watered them, he rolled out his bedroll and laid down to sleep.

The sky was just starting to show signs of light when Sheriff Stillman woke. Off to his left he noticed a sand dune that would provide a bit of high ground. It was not very high, but higher than the surrounding ground.

He went to his saddlebags and got his field glasses, then walked up on the dune. Once he was on top of the dune, he put his field glasses to his eyes and slowly scanned the horizon for evidence of any horses or men.

At first he didn't see anything, but then he noticed something lying on the ground partially hidden behind a yucca plant. He studied it carefully in an effort to figure out what it was. Then it came to him. It was one of the men he had been tracking for the past two days, probably the one that had lost his horse.

Being very suspicious and concerned it might be some kind of a trap, Stillman began scanning the area again. Off in the distance, he could see some dust. It was too far away to make out what it was, but he felt it was the rest of the fugitives. It looked as if they were leaving one of the outlaws behind.

Stillman returned to his camp and packed up his supplies. He mounted up and started off across the barren land again. He moved slowly so his horses didn't kick up a lot of dust. He didn't want to be spotted by those who had gone ahead, nor did he want to be seen by the one they left behind.

When he got close to the one who had been left behind, he dismounted and drew his gun. With the reins of his horse in one hand and his gun in the other, he carefully moved closer to the outlaw. When he was only a few feet away, it was clear the outlaw was not going to cause him any trouble. His lips were swollen and his face was sunburned almost to the point where he was unrecognizable. He had escaped from the jailhouse without a hat, the one thing no cowboy would be without.

Stillman knelt down beside the outlaw. He was still alive, but just barely. There was nothing Stillman could do for him. He would be dead soon.

"Water, please," the outlaw begged, his voice in a whisper and his eyes pleading for help.

"Can't spare it. You shouldn't have killed my deputy."

"Don't leave me here to die."

"Got no choice. I can't let the others get away. If you're still alive when I come back, I'll help yah."

The outlaw knew he had set his course and there was nothing he could do about it now. He would die in this lonely place with no one to say a word or two over him. He turned his head away and closed his eyes.

Stillman stood up, then turned around and walked to his horses. He had a canteen that had just a little water left in it. He took the canteen off his saddle and took it over to the man.

"This might get you through the day if you're careful," he said as he set the canteen next to the outlaw.

Once again, Stillman returned to his horses. He mounted up and started off after the rest of the outlaws. He never once turned and looked back. There was no need to look back. The man would most likely die before the sun set.

Stillman continued to ride along the trail left by the outlaws. He no longer had any idea where the fugitives were going. They had changed direction. All he knew for sure was there was nothing out there for many miles. If they made it to the nearest water hole, they would be lucky.

Suddenly there was the sound of a gunshot. Stillman reined up and quickly jumped off his horse. He ducked down behind a bush and looked out across the dry, hot prairie. He could not see anything because of a small rise in the land ahead of him.

Carefully, he led his horses forward. He kept his gun firmly gripped in his hand, ready for whatever might happen. When he got close to the top of the rise, he tied his horses to a bush then crawled the rest of the way to the top. Looking over the rise to the other side, he could see two of the fugitives he was following standing next to their horses and looking down at the third fugitive. The fugitive on the ground had been shot in the chest and looked as if he were dead. Stillman was close enough he could hear what was going on.

"What the hell did you do that for, Will?"

Stillman recognized the man as Will Sommers. He was a known killer and bank robber. The other man was just a kid. His name was John Truman. He was known to be good with a gun. He had been in a couple of gunfights, but up to now was not wanted for anything that Stillman knew of. Now he was wanted for the murder of his deputy.

"The damn idiot was stealin' water, kid," he retorted.

"Did you have to kill him?"

"Sure did. The way he was going through the water, he'd have drunk it all. You want to be out here without no water?"

"No," John replied softly as he looked down at the ground.

"Then enough said. We best get moving. We've wasted enough time out here."

"Will, are we going to make it?"

"We are if you can keep up. Otherwise, I'll leave you here, too."

Stillman thought about taking them right here and now, but to do so was risky. He didn't have a good position and he couldn't see them all that well. He might be able to get one of them, but to take them both would be difficult at best. The heavy dry brush of the dry desert would give them good cover and the opportunity to slip away.

"Come on, kid. Walk your horse for awhile," Will said as they started off again. "He'll last better."

Stillman watched them as they began walking away from him. He might have stood a chance if they had mounted up, but with their horses between them and him made it too difficult to surprise them enough to take them prisoners. He wanted these two alive, if possible.

Stillman waited until they were well on their way before he returned to his horses. He took the reins in his hands and began walking his horses.

He spent the better part of the afternoon walking along the trail the two remaining fugitives were leaving. He was careful to keep an eye out for any change in the pattern of their pace or stride. Even a simple change might indicate that they were planning something, or they knew he was not far behind them.

As darkness came upon the land, the two fugitives stopped to set up camp. They built a small fire and made some coffee and cooked a little bacon.

Stillman tied his horses some distance from their camp and worked his way in closer. He sat down in the darkness in a place where he could watch them. There was nothing he could do now but wait. He knew Will was fast and deadly with a gun. The kid he only knew by reputation, but that was enough to make him not want to take any chances.

As the night dragged on, the outlaws let the fire burn down to red coals and a few yellow flames that would flicker up from time to time. They must have thought no one was on their trail as they both laid down near the fire and slept.

As Stillman watched them, a plan developed in his head. It was late into the night when Stillman decided to make his move. He wanted them alive, but he also wanted all the fight out of them. He would simply leave them without horses or water. They would have little choice but to follow him and try to get them back, or go on without horses or water. Either way, they would soon be in no shape to put up much of a fight at which time he would take them prisoner and take them back to jail.

He slowly and quietly slipped around to where they had their horses tied. He gently rubbed the nose of each of the horses to keep them quiet while he carefully untied them. Once he had the horses free of the bush, he slowly walked them out away from the camp. As soon as he was far enough away, he turned and walked them in a wide circle to where he had left his horses.

Stillman now had all the horses and the fugitives were on foot. He also noticed he had their water supply. They had left their canteens on their saddles and had failed to take the saddles off their horses. Things were working out better than he had hoped.

There was no doubt in Stillman's mind the outlaws would try to get their horses back and would try to kill him in the process. As long as they were on foot and had no water, Stillman had the upper hand. However, it was not going to be easy keeping his advantage. They would follow the tracks of their horses.

Now all Stillman had to do was to pack up. The morning light had not even started to appear in the eastern sky when Sheriff Stillman began his walk back the way he had come. He wasn't entirely sure his plan would work, but he knew if he could get back to the rise in the landscape, he would be able to see if they were coming after him.

When the sun finally broke over the horizon, Stillman had left a good distance between him and the fugitives. He found a place where he could see for some distance. He tied up the horses and took out his field glasses and scanned the country behind him.

Sure enough, Will Sommers and John Truman were following the trail he was leaving. It was clear by the way Will was walking and the look on his face that he was mad as hell. The kid was almost cowering as he walked just a little behind Will. He might have been afraid Sommers would take out their misfortune on him.

Stillman once again started off with the horses. He moved at a pretty good pace. Not so fast as to leave them further behind, but fast enough to keep them from gaining on him. He also knew if he was not too far ahead of them, they would see him as he crossed over the next little rise. He felt that would give them some incentive to continue after him. It was Stillman's goal to get to the rise as quickly as possible where he could carry out the rest of his plan.

It was getting on toward dark when Stillman reached the rise. He led the horses up the rise and stopped on top. He then looked back to see if Sommers and Truman were still following him. They were, but they were slowing down and the hard fast walk across the dry land under the hot blazing sun was taking its toll on them. He also noticed they quickly ducked behind some tall shrubs when they saw he had stopped. Stillman smiled as he thought about them taking his bait.

It was now time to set the trap. After a long hard day of crossing the arid land they would be tired and thirsty. They would also be weak and might just take chances they normally would not take.

With night so close, Stillman was sure they would wait until darkness was covering the land before they would attack him and try to take back their horses and his water.

Since Stillman knew where they were, he built a small fire just over the rise. They would be able to see the glow of the fire, but not the fire itself or him.

After he tied the horses off a little way from his camp, Stillman dug a shallow hole in the soft dirt and buried three of the full canteens under a Yucca plant. He left the two partially empty canteens on the horses. He felt that if his plan didn't work, they would not have enough water to make it across the barren land.

He returned to his fire and made coffee and cooked his bacon. He listened very carefully for any noise that might not be part of the usual noises of the night. Although he was convinced they would not attack him until they thought he was asleep, he still had to be ready for anything.

As soon as he had eaten, he built up a mound of sand and covered it with his blanket. When he was satisfied that in the dark it looked like a person sleeping, he slipped back away from the fire and hid behind some bushes. His gun in his hand, he settled in to wait for Sommers and Truman to make their move.

It had been dark for well over two hours before Stillman heard a twig snap off to his right, then silence. He thought he could hear some whispering, but was not sure. He knew they were close.

Suddenly, Sommers stepped out of the darkness near the campfire and put two quick shots into the blanket. The kid seemed pleased that his big friend had killed the man who had been trailing them. That is until he realized there was no one under the blanket, just a pile of sand.

"Drop the gun, Sommers," Stillman demanded from his hiding place.

Sommers didn't move for a couple of seconds, then instantly turned and fired a shot toward the bush. Stillman fired a shot back at Sommers as he dove for cover behind some Yucca plants. When Stillman saw he had hit Sommers, he quickly turned and fire two shots at Truman.

Sommers' shot had missed Stillman, but he was not so lucky. Stillman's shot hit

Sommers in the upper leg shattering the bone. However, he was not out of the fight. He fired two more shots into the bush Stillman had been hiding behind, but it was too late. Stillman had rolled off to the side into a little dip in the sandy ground. The shots went over his head.

"Did you get him?" The kid asked.

"How the hell do I know," Sommers growled, then he tried to drag himself toward a bush.

Suddenly a shot ran out. The bullet hit the ground just in front of Sommers kicking up dirt in front of him. He froze where he lay.

"Give it up," Stillman shouted. "I've got you in my sights. You can't get to cover before I can kill you."

Sommers looked toward Truman. He knew it was over. There was nothing he could do now. He would wait until an opportunity presented itself.

"Stand up and put your hands up, kid," Stillman said.

Truman looked at Sommers as if he was looking to him to tell him what he should do.

"Do as he says," Sommers insisted, then he laid down as the pain in his leg was becoming almost too much for him.

Truman tossed his gun out where Stillman would be able to see it. He then put his hands up and stood up where Stillman could see him.

Stillman was no fool. He had been a lawman for a long time. Sommers may have acted like he was giving up, but Stillman knew that as long as he was alive he was still dangerous.

"Kid, walk toward me," Stillman said.

The kid looked down at Sommers as if he was looking for direction, but he got none. He turned and looked back toward where Stillman was still hiding. He then slowly started walking toward Stillman with his hands in the air.

Stillman watched as the kid moved closer and closer. He stood up and stepped sideways which put the kid directly in between him and Sommers. He was using the kid as a shield just in case Sommers decided he wanted to try something.

"Stop," Stillman ordered.

Truman did as he was told. He stopped and stared at the gun Stillman was holding on him.

"Turn around."

Truman looked at Stillman's face, then looked down at the gun again. He then slowly turned around.

Stillman noticed Truman stiffen up as if he was ready to jump. He instantly knew something was about to happen, and since he didn't have a clear view of Sommers at the moment, it was time to make a move.

Stillman jumped to the left just as the kid jumped to the right. A shot was fired, but it missed Stillman. Sommers wasn't so lucky. Stillman's shot ripped a hole in the upper part of Sommers' chest twisting him around.

Stillman turned quickly to see where Truman was and if he had to defend himself from him. He saw the kid lying face down in the sand and not moving.

After a quick look back at Sommers, Stillman stood up. He walked over to the kid and knelt down. He gently rolled him over. There was blood on the side of the kid's head where he had apparently struck his head on a rock when he fell. His shirt also had blood on it near his shoulder. Stillman was sure if the kid survived the blow on the head, he would recover from the gunshot wound to his shoulder.

After Stillman checked and found Sommers to be dead, he went to his packhorse and retrieved some bandages. He first put the kid in leg irons and handcuffs then dressed the kid's wounds.

Stillman dragged Sommers away from the camp and dug a hole where he buried him. He then retrieved the three full canteens he had buried earlier. There was no doubt he would need them to keep the kid alive, that was if he survived the night.

Since Stillman had done all he could for the kid, he fixed his dinner and settled in for the rest of the night. The next morning, he woke before the sun was up. The kid was awake, but he was not moving. Stillman stood up and walked over to him.

"How are you feeling?"

"Not so well," the kid replied as he looked around. "Where's Sommers?"

"Under a pile of rock. You ready to travel?"

"Does it make any difference if I'm not?"

"Not really," Stillman said as he reached down and grabbed the kid by his shirt.

Stillman pulled the kid up on his feet. He was a little unstable, but that was to be expected after last night.

Stillman led the kid to a horse and put him in the saddle. He ran the leg irons under the horse's belly and tied the handcuffs to the saddle horn.

"That should keep you in the saddle," Stillman said as he looked up at the kid.

"I wouldn't try to escape if I was you. You and that horse will die out there without water, and I have all the water."

"What's going to happen to me?" the kid asked.

"I'll take you back to jail. You'll wait there until the circuit judge comes around. We'll have a trial, then you will hang for murdering my deputy."

"How long before the judge gets there?"

"You'll have about three weeks before you get hung. You best spend that time asking the good Lord for forgiveness."

Stillman took the reins of the horse and tied it to the saddle horn of one of the other horses. He then tied the reins of that horse to his packhorse. After he mounted up, he took the lead of his packhorse and began the long trek back to the Texas jailhouse.

THE HOT SPRINGS BANK ROBBERY

It was a typical day in the summer of 1897 in the small town of Hot Springs, in the southern Black Hills. The sun was up and the air was clear. There were only a few fluffy white clouds drifting slowly across the otherwise brilliant blue sky.

The town of Hot Springs had become known for the mineral baths and hot springs in and around the town. People would come to ease their aches and pains by taking long mineral baths at places with names like the Minnekahta Bath House, the Stewart Bath House and the Sulphur Bath House. Some would come just to enjoy the warm clear waters of Evans Plunge.

Hospitals had sprung up in the area including a Veteran's Home and a State Soldier's Home. Hotels were springing up everywhere to accommodate those wishing for relief from their suffering. The town drew all kinds of people from the very rich to the very poor, and from all over the country. All were looking for a miracle. All were looking for a cure to whatever ailed them. Well, maybe not all.

Marshall Sam Tidwell would go down to the Evans Hotel in the early afternoon and sit on one of the benches on the large open porch. The Evans Hotel was located almost directly across the street from the railroad station. He would sit and watch the passengers as they got off the train. He had a keen eye and liked to know who was coming to his town and what reason they might have for being there.

For the most part, it was easy to tell why people were coming here. He would see men, as well as women, using canes and crutches. They were most likely here to get treated for their discomfort. He would see both men and women, and an occasional child, holding handkerchiefs over their mouths and coughing from time to time. They were most likely going to one of the sanitariums for the treatment of their ailment.

However, today was different. It was not those who got off the train that interested Marshall Tidwell on this day. It was the three riders that rode slowly by the front of the hotel.

They didn't look like the typical men who came here. They wore their guns low and tied down on their legs. Their clothes were those of someone who spent a lot of time in the saddle and out on the range, and didn't spend very much time indoors. They had strong healthy mounts that looked like they might be fast and sturdy.

Although they looked like they might be cowpunchers, there was something about them that made Sam suspicious. It may have been the way they looked around. Most people would have thought of them as just taking in their surroundings, but to Sam it was more like they were looking over the town in an effort to decide if what they had in mind would be worth the risk. The more he watched them, the more he felt they were here with no good purpose in mind.

As they passed directly in front of the hotel, one of the riders looked up and saw Marshall Tidwell watching them. The man stared back at the Marshall as he slowly rode by, then smiled as he reached up and touched the brim of his hat and nodded slightly.

Sam nodded slightly in return, but continued to watch the riders until they disappeared around a corner. Sam continued to mentally size up the riders even after they were out of sight. They were well armed and looked as if they might know how to use the weapons they carried.

Sam immediately got up and walked down the street to his office. As he walked through the door, he found Billy tacking some wanted posters up on the wall.

Billy was not a real deputy. He was a young man who liked to hang around the Marshall's office and do a few chores like sweeping, running errands and making coffee. Sam knew Billy wasn't the smartest young man around town, but he was dependable and would do as he was told as long as it was made clear what he was to do.

"Billy, did you happen to see the three riders that just came into town?"

"No, sir. I was sortin' the mail and gettin' these here posters up."

"They looked like they were headed to the Ferguson Hotel. I want you to go over there and see if you can find out what their names are. Now, don't you try to talk to them. You just ask the desk clerk for their names. You understand?"

"Yes, sir. Just get their names from the desk clerk."

Sam nodded, then watched as Billy grabbed his hat off the peg next to the door and left the office. As soon as Billy was gone, Sam took a look at the new posters that had come in on the train. He didn't recognize any of them, but he filed them away in the back of his mind. He then sat down behind his desk. He propped his feet up and leaned back in his chair as he thought about the three riders.

It wasn't very long before Billy returned. He seemed rather excited, but that was the way he was whenever he got to do any real 'deputy type work', as he called it.

"Well, I got what you wanted," Billy said rather proud of himself.

"Are you going to tell me?"

"Oh, sure. The three riders did just what you said they would do. They checked in the Ferguson Hotel."

"Billy, what names did they use," Sam asked, getting just a little impatient with him.

"Oh, yeah. The desk clerk told me the one who seemed to be in charge called hisself Frank Millett. The other older fella called hisself Clay Hunter, and the younger one was Nathan Hunter."

"I've heard of Frank Millett, but I don't know the others," Sam said thoughtfully.

"How is it you know of Millett. He a outlaw or somethin'," Billy asked.

"Yeah. I think if you get to looking through some of those older posters, you might find something on him."

"That what you want me to do?"

"No," Sam replied thoughtfully.

"What you goin' to do? You goin' to arrest him?"

"I might have to, but for now I think I'll just keep an eye on him."

"Can I help?"

"You sure can, Billy. I want you to go over to Ma Baker's rooming house and sit on her porch. I want to know when those three leave the hotel. Don't you do anything except watch. You just let me know when they leave the hotel."

"I understand. Just keep watch and let you know when they leave."

"That's right," Sam said. "Now get going,"

Sam watched as Billy left the office, again. He sat back down behind his desk and opened one of the lower drawers. He pulled out a stack of old wanted posters and started sorting through them. It wasn't long before he came across the poster for Frank Millett. There was a reward for Frank. It was a good sum of money, five hundred dollars. He was wanted for killing a guard at a bank in eastern South Dakota. As far as Sam was concerned, he was not wanted here.

This bit of information gave Sam a good idea as to why these three men were here. If they killed a guard at a bank, there was a good possibility they were planning to rob a bank in Hot Springs.

Sam got up and walked outdoors. He stood in front of his office for a moment or two as he looked up and down the street. He was trying to decide what he should do next. His real deputy, Will Parker, was out in the hills somewhere serving papers on a miner who had caused some damage to one of the hotels while he was in town to let off some steam. Sam didn't expect Parker back before dark, maybe not until morning.

It wouldn't be long before the sun would set. Sam thought it would be best if he went over to Ma Baker's rooming house and had some dinner. After that he would let Billy go home and he would take over keeping an eye on the riders.

Sam left his office and began walking toward Ma Baker's rooming house. As he walked by the First National Bank, he noticed a poster in the window. He stopped and looked at it. It had been there for some time, but today was the first time it registered in his mind. The poster read, "Largest bank in the Southern Black Hills".

The longer Sam stared at the poster, the more he became convinced it was the reason the three riders had come to town. The fact that one of them was already known to have been involved in a bank robbery gave support to Sam's thoughts about their purpose for being in Hot Springs.

Sam continued his walk toward Ma Baker's rooming house. He was deep in thought when he noticed Billy running toward him.

"What's up, Billy?"

"Them three just left the Ferguson Hotel, and, and they was headed over to the saloon," Billy said excitedly.

"Okay. You run over to the office and get a shotgun. I want you outside the saloon doors. I want you to be ready if something happens, but I don't want anyone inside the saloon to see you. You understand?"

"Yes, sir. You want me to cover you. Right?"

"That's right, Billy. Now get going and don't stop for anyone."

"Yes, sir," Billy replied, then turned and dashed off toward the Marshall's office.

Sam watched as Billy ran down the street. As soon as he was out of sight, he drew his gun from his holster and checked it. He had no intentions of getting into a gunfight with these men, but needed to be ready just in case.

When Sam arrived at the saloon, he stopped at the swinging doors and looked inside. There were a number of people in the saloon tonight. Some were playing cards at the tables while others were just sitting around talking and drinking. He noticed the three riders he was looking for were standing at the bar. They had their backs to the bar and seemed to be just looking around to see what was going on.

Sam took a deep breath and then stepped into the saloon. No one seemed to pay any attention to him until he walked up to the end of the bar.

"Howdy, Marshall," the barkeep said.

Sam noticed the three men quickly turned their heads and looked at him. They didn't say anything. They just looked him over as if sizing him up.

"Howdy, Stan," Sam replied as casually as possible. "How's it going tonight?"

"Not bad. It's been pretty quiet tonight."

"Good, let's keep it that way."

"I'll sure try," Stan replied with a smile.

"I'll see you later," Sam said then turned around and walked out of the saloon.

Just as he stepped through the door, he saw Billy standing off to the side with a shotgun in his hands. Sam smiled at him and nodded so Billy would know he had done a good job.

"Come on, Billy," Sam said as he started down the street toward the Marshall's office.

"Where we goin'?"

"Back to the office."

"Ain't you goin' to arrest them?"

"Not tonight."

"Why?"

"Because they haven't done anything I can arrest them for."

Billy nodded that he understood, but Sam was sure he didn't. Billy had a picture in his mind that it was a marshal's job to arrest people. He couldn't understand the full range of duties a town marshal had, or that a marshal couldn't arrest people on a whim.

Once they arrived back at the Marshall's office, Sam took the shotgun from Billy and put it back in the gun rack on the wall. He then sat down at his desk while Billy sat down in a chair near the desk.

"We goin' to keep watch of them fellas?" Billy asked.

"Not any more tonight. Billy, do you think you could be back here before the sun comes up?"

"Sure," he said excitedly.

"Good. I want you here before the sun comes up. I want you to be ready to do something for me."

"Okay. What do you want me to do?"

"That will depend on whether or not Will gets back."

"Okay. I'll be here," Billy assured him.

Sam didn't say anything more. He had a pretty good idea what was going through Billy's mind.

"Billy, you can go get some rest. You'll need all the rest you can get come morning."

"Okay," Billy replied as he stood up and started out the door.

When Billy got to the door, he stopped and turned around. He stood looking at the floor and didn't say anything.

"What is it Billy?"

"I was just wonderin', do you want me to bring my gun?"

Sam looked at Billy's face. He wasn't sure just what he should say, but if Will didn't get back he might need Billy's gun if for nothing more than for backup.

"Yes, Billy. Bring your gun with you. We may need it."

Billy smiled, then turned and quickly left the office. Sam looked at the door for a long time. He was concerned about having Billy help him if the three riders were in town to rob the bank. Billy was a good man when he had instructions in detail. He was even a fair shot with a handgun or rifle, but he wasn't sure how he would react if it turned into a running gun battle and he had to make split second decisions.

It was too late for him to worry about it now. He needed to get some rest. If Will didn't get back, it could prove to be an interesting day. Sam locked up the office on his way out. He walked down the street to Ma Baker's rooming house where he had a room.

As he passed the saloon, he took a moment to look in. The three riders were not there. He was sure they were getting their sleep before they hit the bank. There was little doubt in Sam's mind that they would hit the bank in the morning when it opened, and when the streets would be nearly empty. At least for that he could be thankful.

Sam left the saloon and went directly to his room. He laid down on his bed and put his hands behind his head. He found it difficult to go to sleep. His mind was cluttered with what might happen in the morning. It took a while before he finally dozed off.

* * * *

It was still dark outside when Sam woke. He laid in bed and wondered what this day was going to bring. He had convinced himself that Frank Millett and his two partners were in town to do no good. He had no proof, but he could feel it in his bones. Today, someone was going to die. The only question was who?

Sam got up and got ready to go to work. He strapped on his six gun and left his room for Ma Baker's kitchen. The kitchen was empty except for Ma Baker who was preparing breakfast for her guests.

"Morning, Marshall. You're up mighty early," Ma Baker said.

"Morning, Ma," Sam replied.

"You hungry?"

"Not really. I got to get over to the office. Just a cup of coffee, please."

"You expectin' trouble?" she asked as she poured him a cup of steaming hot coffee.

"Might be," Sam replied as he reached out and took the cup.

"You should eat something. Let me fix you a roll to take with you."

"Thanks."

Sam took a sip of the coffee while he waited for Ma Baker to wrap hot breakfast rolls in a cloth napkin.

"I put a couple of rolls in there for you," she said as she handed the package to him. "Go ahead and take the cup. You can bring it back later."

Sam nodded a thank you, then turned and left the kitchen.

The sky was starting to get light as Sam walked toward his office. The air was a little cool this morning, but he didn't really notice. He was too busy thinking about what might happen this morning.

When he arrived at his office, he noticed that there was a light in the window. He was sure he had blown out the lantern last night.

The door was slightly ajar. As he passed by the window he saw Billy in the office. It looked as if he was making coffee. Sam walked in, went directly to his desk and set his cup down.

"Mornin', sir," Billy said. "I'm makin' coffee."

"Morning, Billy. I see you're wearing your gun."

"Yes, sir. You told me to bring it," Billy replied, his face showing he might have misunderstood Sam.

"You'll need more than a gun this morning," Sam said as he pulled open the center drawer of his desk.

Sam reached in and pulled out a deputy badge. He held it out to Billy.

"You're going to need this."

Billy looked at the badge for a moment or two, then reached out and took it. He looked at Sam for a second before he pinned the badge on his shirt above his left breast pocket.

"Will didn't get back last night. I need you to help me."

"Yes, sir," Billy replied as he waited for instructions.

"You know the firewood box that sets along side the General Mercantile store?"

"Yes, sir."

"I want you to take a shotgun and go over there. I want you to hide behind the box and keep an eye on the bank. I don't want you to do anything unless I say so. Do you understand?"

"Yes, sir. What you goin' to do?"

"I'll be on the other side of the store."

"Oh."

"Don't shoot unless I do. And go down the alley to get there so no one will see you."

"Okay. You want me to go now?"

"Yes, and take one of those rolls with you. You may be there awhile. I'll be along shortly."

Billy took a shotgun from the gun rack, checked it, then picked up a roll on his way out of the office. Sam sat down at his desk and penned a note to Will, just in case he got in before the trouble started. He ate the remaining roll and then left the office.

By this time the sun had come up over the surrounding hills, the day was starting to warm up. The streets were still pretty quiet, but there was some activity around a few of the stores as the owners prepared to open for business.

As Sam passed behind the general store, he noticed Billy kneeling down behind the firewood box. He was watching the front of the bank very carefully. He had to smile to himself when he saw how seriously Billy took the job of deputy, but then he should. Today was a day to be serious.

Once Sam was in position, he leaned back against the store and waited as he hid behind a rain barrel. Every few minutes Sam would look out from behind the corner of the building and look up and down the street. It seemed as if it was taking forever for something to happen. He was growing impatient. He was sure Billy was growing impatient, too.

Sam took another look out from his hiding place. This time he saw Mr. R.B. Bracket, the president of the bank, coming down the street. A quick glance at his pocket watch told him it was getting close to the time when the bank would open.

Mr. Bracket had no more than unlocked the front door and gone inside when Sam heard the sounds of horses slowly plodding down the hard dirt street.

Sam drew back out of sight behind the rain barrel and watched as the horses moved past. The rider of the lead horse was none other then Frank Millett. Clay and Nathan Hunter followed closely behind him.

As soon as they were past him, Sam peeked out from the corner of the store. He saw them rein up in front of the bank and slowly look around.

When Frank stepped down off his horse, Clay did the same. Nathan stayed sitting in the saddle. Clay and Frank handed Nathan the reins to their horses, then stepped up on the boardwalk in front of the bank. As Frank reached for the doorknob of the bank door with one hand, he pulled his gun from his holster with the other. Clay drew his gun, took a quick look around before following Frank into the bank. Nathan slipped his gun out of his holster and casually laid it in his lap so he would be ready. He sat in the saddle and looked around to make sure all was quiet.

Sam took a quick check of his gun. There was no doubt things were about to happen and would happen very quickly. It was also running through Sam's mind he was outnumbered. He just hoped Billy was going to be enough help. It was the waiting that was so nerve racking, but Sam and Billy would not have to wait much longer.

Suddenly, the door to the bank flew open and Frank and Clay came running out. They each had two bags of money from the bank. They ran straight to their horses, but the horses were excited. They had trouble getting hold of their reins because the horses were prancing around nervously.

"Hold it right there," Sam yelled from the corner of the store.

As quick as lightning, Frank fired the first shot toward the corner of the store. It hit just above Sam's head splitting and scattering bits of wood from the building. The sudden commotion and the loud report of Frank's gunshot made Nathan's horse take off down the street. Nathan failed to let go of the reins to Frank and Clay's horses, leaving the men on foot in front of the bank.

As Nathan's horse ran wildly past the corner of the store where Billy had been hiding, Billy stepped out and fired one shot from his shotgun. The blast of the shotgun took Nathan right out of the saddle, dumping him in the dirt while the horses high tailed it on down the street.

Meanwhile, Clay and Frank ducked around the corner of the bank while exchanging shots with Sam. Almost as quickly as the shooting had begun, it had stopped.

Sam had seen Frank and Clay disappear behind the row of buildings on the other side of the street. He was not completely sure, but he thought he might have hit one of them.

"Billy," Sam called out.

"Yeah?"

"You okay?"

"Yeah. I got one of 'um."

"Keep an eye out. Let me know if either of the other two go down your way behind the buildings."

"Yes, sir."

Billy moved back behind the firewood box and watched between the buildings while Sam ran across the street to the front of the bank.

Sam leaned up against the front of the bank. As he took a deep breath, he happened to glance down at the boardwalk. He noticed a few drops of fresh blood. He had hit one of them in the exchange of gunfire, but apparently not seriously enough to stop him.

He took another deep breath, then slowly looked around the corner of the bank toward the back alley. He didn't see anyone.

"Billy?"

"Yes, sir?"

"Did you see anyone go that way?"

"No, sir."

"Get over here."

Billy quickly jumped up from his hiding place and ran across the street. As soon as he was leaning up against the front of the bank next to Sam, he looked back down the street.

"I got one of 'um."

"Yeah, I see."

"Is he dead?"

"Not sure, but he's out of the fight," Sam said. "You did a good job. Now all we have to do is get the other two."

"What do you want me to do?"

"I want you to follow me and keep my back covered. You understand?"

"Yes, sir."

Sam took another look around the corner of the bank. As soon as he was sure it was clear, he ran around the corner and along the side of the bank to the back corner. He glanced back to see if Billy was watching.

He motioned for Billy to join him. Billy ran up next to Sam and waited for instruction.

"Keep me covered," Sam said then darted out around the corner behind the building.

Sam worked his way along the back of the buildings. Every once in a while he would see fresh blood on the ground. From the direction that they were going, he was pretty sure they were headed for Jensen's Livery Stable to get horses.

Just as he came around the corner where he could see the front of Jensen's Livery Stable, he saw the door opening. Frank came out leading a horse, but before he could mount up Sam fired a shot at him. His bullet caught Frank in the side and knocked him to the ground.

"Give it up," Sam yelled.

Several shots rang out causing Sam to duck back behind the corner of the building. The shots gave Frank cover, allowing him to scramble back into the livery stable.

"Give it up," Sam called out, again.

"What for, so you can hang us?"

"You'll get a fair trial."

"Sure, then you'll hang us."

"You're both wounded. You might as well give it up."

"Over my dead body," Frank yelled back defiantly.

Sam was not in the best of positions. From where he was, it could prove to be a long standoff.

Just then the doors of the livery stable opened again. Several horses that where tightly grouped together came out very slowly. Sam could see someone's legs below the horses. Whoever it was he was using the horses for cover in order to get away.

Sam stepped out and fired two quick shots in the air as he yelled. The horses broke and ran. He saw Clay sprint for cover around the corner. It happened so quickly Sam was unable to get a shot off at him.

"Keep Frank pinned in the livery stable," Sam told Billy, then ran off after Clay.

The chase after Clay quickly turned into a running gunfight. They ducked in and out of doorways and around corners of buildings as Sam pursued Clay, occasionally firing shots at each other. Sam lost track of Clay for a moment or two when he stopped to reload his gun. He didn't see where Clay had gone, but he was sure he was close to a small house only a few yards away.

The house had some bushes around it and along a fence. It made it difficult for Sam to see. There were a number of places where Clay could be hiding near the house.

Sam moved slowly and carefully toward the small house, his eyes continually moving in the hope of seeing Clay before it was too late. As he moved up close to the house something flashed in the glass window. Sam turned quickly as he dove for cover. A shot was fired and the bullet slammed into the side of the house, just missing Sam.

Instinctively, Sam returned fire. He fired two quick shots into a large bush near the front gate. He thought he heard the sound of someone in pain. He continued to focus his attention on the bush. In a couple of seconds, he noticed some movement. Keeping his gun pointed at the bush, he watched.

After a minute or two, he saw Clay slowly stagger out from behind the bush. His eyes were glazed over and he wobbled as he tried to walk. He still had his gun in his hand, but his hand was at his side. Clay staggered a few more steps, then stopped and looked at Sam. He looked as if he was trying to raise his gun. Instead, his knees buckled and he fell into the bush. His gun dropped from his hand, then all movement stopped.

Sam cautiously walked over to him. Clay would never try to rob a bank again, he was dead.

Sam immediately turned around and ran back toward the livery stable. He found Billy patiently waiting where he had been left.

"Has he tried to leave?" Sam asked.

"No, sir. There ain't been a sound out of there," Billy said. "You think he's dead?"

"He might be, but I wouldn't count on it."

"You think he's waitin' for us to go in after him?"

"Could be."

"What yah goin' to do?"

"Think about it for a minute," Sam replied.

Billy just looked at Sam. He didn't say anything. He was wondering what Sam was thinking about.

"Frank Millett," Sam called out, then waited.

There was no answer, so he called out again. There was still no answer.

Sam looked at Billy. He wasn't sure how to proceed from here. He needed good reliable backup if he was going to try to get Frank out of the livery stable.

"Billy, I need you to cover me. I want you to run over there behind the water trough and keep your gun on the door. I'll cover you."

"Yes, sir."

Billy stood up and quickly ran across the open ground toward the water trough. He dove in behind the trough, then swung around and pointed his shotgun at the door to the stable.

As soon as he looked like he was ready, Sam sprinted across the open space to the front of the stable. He quickly leaned up against the side of the stable near the door. He waited and listened, but he heard nothing.

"Frank?" Sam called out, but again there was no answer.

Sweat began to run down Sam's face. Without any idea as to where Frank might be, or what condition he was in to put up a fight, Sam was left with very little choice. He was going to have to go in and get him out, one way or the other.

Sam looked over at Billy. Billy was watching Sam, looking and waiting for instruction as much as anything.

Sam pointed at the other side of the stable door and motioned for Billy to move there. Billy didn't hesitate, he stood up and ran up to the door and leaned his back against the side of the stable just like Sam. He then stood there waiting to see what Sam was going to do.

Sam looked at Billy. He could see Billy was very nervous, but then he should be. After all, Sam was nervous.

Sam mouthed the words telling Billy that he was going inside the stable, and he was to cover him. Billy nodded he understood. Sam could see Billy's hands shift on the shotgun. Then Billy nodded he was ready.

Sam rushed into the stable and dove into the first stall he came to. He quickly scrambled around to take cover against the heavy boards on the side of the stall.

While he was trying to protect himself, a shot rang out from up above him. The bullet ripped through Sam's shirtsleeve, nicking his arm.

Sam quickly rolled over in an effort to be a moving target. As he came around onto his back, he fired several shots into the floor of the loft. Billy also fired a load of buckshot into the loft. Then there was quiet.

For several seconds there was not a sound. Billy was standing in the door of the stable with his shotgun pointed up toward the loft, and Sam was lying on the floor with his gun pointed toward the loft. Both were ready to shoot.

Suddenly, they saw Frank pull himself upright. He seemed to be looking off into space as his body teetered back and forth for a couple of seconds. He then pitched forward and fell from the loft to the hard dirt floor of the stable below.

Sam laid there for a moment or two with his gun pointed at Frank's body. When Sam finally turned and looked at Billy, he saw him standing in the door with his shotgun pointed at the body.

"You can put it down, Billy," Sam said with a sigh.

Billy looked over at Sam. A smile slowly came over Billy's face. He had done a good job as Sam's deputy. He was pleased with the way he had handled himself, and he was sure Sam was pleased with him, too.

Suddenly, Billy realized there was blood on the sleeve of Sam's shirt. He quickly ran over to Sam.

"You're hurt," he said excitedly.

"I'm fine. You did well, Billy. You can keep the badge as long as you like," Sam said as he stood up.

By this time several people had arrived to see what was going on. One of them was his deputy, Will Parker.

"Will, take care of this. Deputy Billy will help you. I'm going over to the doc's and have my arm looked after."

"I saw the one in the street," Will said.

"Billy got that one. There's another one over by the Blair house. Billy will explain it all," Sam said, then he turned and walked off toward the doctor's office.

THE TALE OF DUFFY McCLUE

It all started a couple of years ago. Yup, it was in the summer of 1883. A man by the name of Duffy McClue rode into the town of Pringle, in the Dakota Territory. That broken down old horse he was a ridin' weren't worth the price of a bullet to put the poor critter out of its misery.

Now, Duffy was a strange sorta fella. He was tall and lean lookin', somethin' akin to a scarecrow. He wore a top hat that was almost as tall as a stovepipe and sorta looked like one though it was bent a might to one side. The black frock coat he wore had seen better days. His boots was so bad wore he had pieces of paper inside to keep the dirt from comin' up through the soles.

The only thin' Duffy had that weren't plum worn out was that six-shooter he carried under his coat. Why, that gun was as clean as could be, and in perfect workin' order. One other thin' I might mention was he knew how and when to use it, but I'm gettin' ahead of myself in this here story.

Duffy, he had a couple of coins rubbin' together. You might say they was burnin' a hole in his pocket. As he rode up in front of the saloon, he sat there just lookin' at them swingin' doors. It 'peared as if he couldn't seem to make up his mind whether to go in and buy himself a drink with his last little bit of money, or whether he should go across the street to the café and get somethin' to fill the hole in his gut.

Well now, Duffy, he turned that old nag around and headed off across the street to the café, and that turned out to be the right decision. It just so happened there was a couple of cowboys who'd been drinkin' a bit too much come out of that saloon at that very moment. They spotted Duffy and commenced to laughin' and pointin' at him.

Now Duffy, he didn't take kindly to bein' laughed at. He stopped that old nag in front of the café and sorta casually slid out of the saddle just as smooth as you please.

After takin' a minute to tie his horse to the hitchin' rail, he turned and looked at them two cowboys. He took a minute or so to size them fellas up. When he was done, he didn't think they was goin' to be much of a problem for him.

"You gents got a problem with somethin'?" Duffy asked as he sorta casually pushed his coat back away from his gun.

I don't think them fellas even seen what Duffy was doin', they was a laughin' so hard.

"Yeah," one of them answered, chucklin'.

"And just what might your problem be?" Duffy asked.

"If you ain't the sorriest lookin' thin' I ever did see, I don't know what is," the cowboy answered, unable to contain his laughter.

"Now, was you talkin' about me, or was you talkin' about my horse?" Duffy asked.

"I was talkin' about you, you old coot."

Now I ain't seen nothin' like it in all my born days. Before the sound of that cowboy's voice faded off in the wind, Duffy pulled that gun of his outa his holster and shoots that cowboy's gun right off his hip.

You shoulda seen the look on that cowboy's face. He was so surprised he couldn't even talk. He just stood there with his mouth hung open like the door on an old outhouse.

"Now, what was you sayin' about the way I look?" Duffy asked polite like.

"Ah , , , ah, nothin' mister. I wasn't sayin' nothin'."

"You got somethin' to say?" Duffy asked the other cowboy.

"Not me. I got nothin' to say."

Duffy watched them two for a little bit, then he turned and went into the café. Them two, why they didn't even move until Duffy was inside the café and sittin' at a table.

Now them cowboys didn't like what Duffy done to them, 'specially the one lost his gun. Duffy had embarrassed them somethin' awful, and he done it right there in the middle of town, too. They had been stung by him and they wasn't about to let him get away with it, but they wasn't just sure what they should do about it, neither. As soon as Duffy was gone, them boys, they mounted up and lit out of town as if their tails was a fire.

Duffy sat in the café and watched them fellas as they rode on out of town. He had a feelin' that he was goin' to have another run in with them 'fore long. There was no doubt that them cowboys was not about to let a sleepin' dog lie.

Duffy, he ordered a couple of eggs, some bacon and coffee, then he commenced to eatin'. He figured after he paid for his breakfast, he would have a little money left.

As he ate, he looked out the window of that café at the saloon across the street. It come to his mind that he might be able to increase his funds if he could get himself into a card game.

Now, Duffy weren't no fool. He knew he didn't have much of a stake. He would have to win the very first round of cards if he was to build himself up any kinda pot.

After he finished his eatin' and paid for his meal, he took his five dollar gold piece that he kept hidden in the linin' of his hat and proceeded across the street to that saloon.

As he entered the saloon, he stopped and stood near the door and kinda looked over the place. Most of the folks in the saloon stopped and looked at him. Most of them had seen what he done earlier to them cowboys.

Well, there was two tables of card playin' folks in the saloon that day. Duffy looked over each of the tables. There was one table had four men sittin' 'round it. They looked like they was playin' for real money. The other table looked like a bunch of poor ranchers that was playin' cards. There was small bettin' goin' on at that one.

It was pretty clear to Duffy which table he should sit down at. He didn't have the money to sit down with them high stakes players, so he moseyed over to the table where the stakes was low.

"You gents mind if I join yah for a bit?" he asked with a pleasant smile.

The four men at the table looked him up and down, then looked at each other. They must of decided he was as harmless and as poor as most of them 'cause they invited him to join 'um.

"Pull up a seat," one of them told him.

"Much obliged," Duffy said as he pulled a chair back and sat down.

"The stakes are limited to a buck a bet with no mor'n' five dollars a pot," one of the other players said.

"That suits me just fine. I ain't got but five dollars anyway," Duffy said with a grin.

Duffy took out his five-dollar gold piece and traded it for five dollars in loose cash. He then commenced to lean back in the chair and wait to be dealt in.

Wouldn't yah know it, after that first round of cards was played out, Duffy's pot had grown to fifteen dollars. After playin' for a few hours, Duffy had a pot in front of him that was darn near close to two hundred dollars by my guess. There was also a couple of less players as he had done cleaned them out.

There was one of them ranchers that was thinkin' Duffy was cheatin' them, but he was smart enough not to say it out loud. He had seen what Duffy had done to them cowboys and wise not to want any part of that.

I'd been sittin' in a corner sippin' on a beer and watchin' what was goin' on. Now I can't say for sure, but I didn't see no signs of cheatin' at that table, and I'd been watchin' pretty close. Duffy just seemed more interested in watchin' the players then he did in his cards. The fella that lost the most, well, he sorta give it away when he had a good hand. He was what some folks would call a easy read. It was easy to tell what he had in his hand by the way he looked.

It weren't long and them folks had had enough. The game broke up after Duffy got most, if not, all their money.

Duffy, he gathered up his winnin's and stuffed it in his coat pocket. He then stacked the cards neat like on the table and stood up. He walked over to the bar, leaned up against it and ordered a drink from the barkeep. As soon as he had his drink, he turned his back to the bar and leaned back against it.

I'll say one thin', Duffy was a patient man. He leaned against that bar slowly sippin' his drink and watchin' them other fellas play. He seemed to take a special interest in one in particular. He looked to Duffy to be a gambler, the kind that you had to watch real close.

It weren't long and Duffy had all them fellas figured out. He knew the weakness of each of them players, includin' that gambler fella. It was time for Duffy to make his move.

Duffy drank down the rest of his drink, then set the glass down on the bar. He walked over to the table where them fellas was playing for some pretty big money.

"You mind if a fella joins in with yah?" Duffy asked.

That gambler looked Duffy up and down. It weren't hard to tell from the look on that gambler's face that he didn't think too much of Duffy. In fact, he sorta turned his nose up at Duffy. I guess he figured that Duffy didn't have the money to play the kind of game they was playin'.

"I don't think you can afford to get in this game," the gambler said.

Duffy just stood there and looked at the gambler for a minute. I don't know just what was goin' on in his head, but he reached into his pocket and pulled out the wade of money he had just won at the other table. He reached out and set that money on the table in front of an empty chair, then stood there looking at that gambler, just waitin'.

Now, I don't know much about people in general, but I know somethin' about gamblers. They'd let the devil himself sit down at their table if they thought for one minute that he might be easy pickin's. That there gambler's eyes lit up like a church on Christmas mornin' at the sight of all that money. I'd be willin' to bet that there gambler was thinkin' Duffy's money was already his.

That gambler looked up at Duffy, smiled a big smile and said, "Have a seat, friend."

Duffy smiled back at the gambler as he reached over and pulled out a chair. He sat down, stacked his money on the table, then leaned back.

Now they commenced to playin' cards. I could see from where I was a sittin' that Duffy played his cards close to his chest. He didn't let on even a little bit what he had, but it didn't take him long to figure out the others. He didn't need to watch anyone at the table but that gambler.

Duffy and that gambler was winnin' most of the hands, but them other fellas would win one once 'n awhile. It seemed to me that they was winnin' just enough to keep 'um in the game.

Duffy, he slowly built up a stack of money in front of him. Each time he won, that gambler looked just a mite bit upset. Up until now, I couldn't see that he was cheatin' none.

It was almost as if he was tryin' to win fair and square, but thin's began to change.

That gambler fella just couldn't seem to get much of Duffy's winnin's, and a good part of it was his. I guess in an effort to get his money back, and to get most of Duffy's, that there gambler began to cheat.

Like I said 'fore, Duffy weren't no fool. He caught on right away that there gambler fella was startin' to cheat. And you could see on Duffy's face that he didn't take kindly to it.

After several hours, Duffy pushed back in his chair, turned and looked at me. I got the feeling he was lookin' for someone to agree with him that there gambler was a cheatin'.

"You," he said to me.

"Yeah?" I said back.

"You gots a marshal in this town," he asked quiet like as if not to cause a commotion.

"No. The last one got himself shot when he tried to arrest a couple of cowboys raisin' a little ruckus in here."

"I was kinda hopin' you had one around."

"The job's open, if'n you're looking for steady work."

"Listen, you goin'a play, or gab with him?" the gambler said, interruptin' Duffy and me.

Duffy slowly turned around and looked that gambler right in the eye. "Just hold your horses there."

"Are you in or out?"

"I'm out for the moment, but I'll be back," Duffy said.

Now that gambler, he didn't want Duffy to leave the table. He knew that a good share of the money that Duffy had was his and he was just startin' to get it back, even if he had to cheat to do it.

Duffy got up from the table and walked over to me. He asked me a few questions, mostly about the marshal's job, then he walked back over to the table and commenced to pickin' up his winnin's, which was considerable.

"Where do you think you're going?" the gambler asked.

"Anywhere I've a mind to. You got any objections?" Duffy asked.

It looked almost as if Duffy was just darin' that gambler to try to stop him from leavin'. That gambler must have decided it wasn't a good idea to press his luck with Duffy. He had seen how fast he was with a gun.

"Don't you worry none, I'll be back in a bit. I got some business to 'tend to. We can pick up this game after dinner," Duffy said with a smile.

That gambler didn't like it much, but he figured that he didn't have much of a choice. He sat there and watched as Duffy walked out of that saloon.

Duffy went off across the street to the general store and bought himself some new clothes. He then went over to the barbershop where he got himself a shave and had his mustache trimmed a mite. He got himself a bath, too.

After a couple of hours, Duffy McClue returned to the saloon, only he weren't Duffy McClue no more, he was Marshall McClue.

Marshall McClue come strollin' into that saloon just as smart as you please. He walked up to that gambler fella and stood there lookin' down at him. Yah know, I don't think that gambler fella realized right away who he was.

"We don't 'llow cheatin' in this here town," Duffy said as he looked down at the gambler.

"Who the hell you think you are?" the gambler spat out.

Duffy didn't say nothin', he simply pulled back his new jacket and showed that bright shiny star on his chest to that gambler.

Now that gambler fella, he looked up at Duffy as if he was wantin' to kill him. He pushed back his chair and stood up. He stepped back away from the table and looked like he might be lookin' for a fight.

"I'd take a second to think about what's goin' on in your head, if I was you," Duffy said sorta quiet like. "It ain't worth dyin' over a few hundred dollars."

That gambler fella, he swallowed hard, then glanced at the money he still had on the table. He commenced to thinkin' about what Duffy had done earlier. I guess he didn't figure that he had much of a chance agin' Duffy 'cause he let his coat fall back over his gun. He then stepped toward that table. As he leaned over to pick up his money, he stopped suddenly at the sound of Duffy's voice.

"Leave it," Duffy said.

That gambler, he turned his head and looked at Duffy. He just sorta froze right there in his tracks. He wanted that money real bad.

"You can't do that," the gambler said.

"You won most of that money by cheatin'. I plan to make sure it gets back to them that it rightly belongs to."

"You can't do this," the gambler protested again.

"I not only can, I'm doin' it. You go get your horse and you get out of town while you still can. I suggest you don't come back," Duffy said.

That gambler fella looked Duffy right in the eye. I was sure that this was goin' to turn into a gunfight, but all of a sudden that gambler looked around the room. He could see that everyone there was waitin' to see if he was goin' to draw against the town's new marshal.

"You'll wish you'd never done this," the gambler threatened, then he took off out the door.

Everyone watched as that gambler stormed out of the saloon and turned down the street toward the livery barn. As soon as he was gone, they turned back and looked at Duffy. They all looked like they was expectin' him to say somethin'.

Duffy looked around at the men in the room. He then turned and looked at me. I sorta nodded to let him know that what he'd done was good and that maybe he should say somethin' to these good folks.

Duffy turned back around and said, "There ain't goin' to be no cheatin' in this town. If'n you cheat, you can expect to have your winnin's taken, and you'll be run out of town."

Duffy then commenced to dole out the money that the gambler had left to the men who had been sittin' at the table with him. Once that was done, all those who had been gamblin' took their money and left the saloon. Duffy walked up to the bar and ordered himself a drink. I sorta moved up along side him.

"You goin' to stop gamblin' in town, Marshall?" I asked.

"No. I'm just goin' ta stop cheatin'. If they can't win fair and square, they hadn't outta be playin'."

"Now that you're the Marshall, what you goin' to do about them cowboys?"

"What cowboys?" he asked.

"The ones you made fools out of this mornin'."

"I don't think I'll have any trouble with them."

"You will. I'd watch my back if I was you."

Duffy sipped on his drink as he looked at me. I got the feelin' that he was a mullin' over what I had said.

I left Duffy to consider what I'd said. It wasn't 'til just a little 'for dark that I went back to the saloon.

On my way to the saloon, I walked by the stable. I noticed a couple of horses tied out front I'd seen earlier. They was the same horses them cowboys had been ridin' this mornin'. I could also hear voices comin' from near the stable. I sorta drifted over that a way to get a listen.

Now I didn't hear all that was said, but I got enough to get the gist of what they was a plannin'. It seems them cowboys had run into that gambler fella. Amongst the three of them, they was plannin' on killin' the town's new Marshall.

I hurried over to the saloon to let the Marshall know about it. When I come into the saloon, I saw Duffy sittin' in a chair with his back agin' the wall. He was playin' cards all by himself, but he was watchin' what was goin' on 'round the saloon.

"I just come by to let you know that there gambler fella and them two cowboys you had a run-in with this mornin' are comin' after yah," I said.

Duffy looked up sorta casual like and said, "When?"

"Now. They plan to get yah cornered in here."

"Thanks," he said sorta casual like. "You best find a safe place to go."

I moved off across the room into a corner where I'd most likely be out of harm's way. Duffy, he got up and walked over to the bar.

"You got a scattergun under that bar?" Duffy asked the barkeep.

"Sure do, Marshall," the barkeep replied with a smile.

"I want it."

The barkeep, he didn't hesitate one second. He reached down under that bar and came up with that scattergun. He handed it to Duffy then stood back to watch.

Duffy took that scattergun and went back to the corner where he had been sittin'. He checked it to make sure that it was loaded, then pulled a chair up close. He set that gun across the arms of that there chair so it was in easy reach.

Duffy sits back down in his chair and drew his pistol out of his holster and laid it across his lap. It was clear what he was goin' to do. He was ready, and he weren't goin' to spend a whole lot of time worrin' himself while he waited.

Duffy picked up the deck of cards that was on the table and commenced to playin' all by himself. He didn't really look like he was payin' much attention, but if he'd been a dog his ears woulda been stickin' straight up. He was listenin' to every little sound, and he was thinkin' real hard. There was no doubt in his mind that they was plannin' on comin' at him from all directions.

It was just shortly after dark that thin's commenced to happen. One of them cowboys come in through the front door while the other sorta hid himself near the front window. The gambler fella, he was tryin' to sneak in the back.

Duffy, he didn't miss a thin'. He saw that cowboy's gun just outside the window and he heard that gambler fella step on a loose plank on the saloon floor.

Now, you got to remember that I was a duckin' the lead that started to fly when that first cowboy come chargin' in the door. So this may not'ta been exactly how it all happened.

Duffy dropped the cards he had in his hand. When his hand came back up, it was full of shotgun. That old double barrel scattergun went off, one barrel right after the other. The first shot hit the first cowboy right square in the chest and sent him flyin' right back out the door.

The second round hit right near the edge of the front window where that other cowboy was tryin' not to be seen. Some of that buckshot musta hit him good 'cause I heard a mighty painful yelp from him.

Duffy, he dropped that scattergun real quick like, almost as if it was too hot to hold onto. He then grabbed up that six shooter of his and dove for the floor just as a pistol shot hit the back of the chair he'd been sittin' in.

Duffy rolled over and commenced to shootin' at that gambler fella. He didn't hit him with the first shot or two, but he sure scared the hell out'ta him. That gambler was scramblin' like crazy to get out of there, but on the third or fourth shot Duffy caught him in the leg. That gambler fella, he went a crashin' to the floor like a sack of potatoes.

When Duffy got to his feet, he walked over to that gambler. He stood over him with his gun pointed right at him, almost darin' him to try somethin'.

That gambler was in a might bit of pain and in no condition to carry on the fight. When he looked up and saw Duffy standin' over him, ready to shoot him, he began to beggin' for his life.

"I ain't goin' to kill you, at least not right away. I'm goin' to give you five minutes to get out of town. If you ain't out of town by then, I'll shoot you down just like the rattlesnake you are," Duffy said.

"But my leg?" the gambler cried.

"You had two mighty good ones 'fore you decided to kill me. You shoulda left then. Now, you got one good leg. I suggest you find a way to get out of town on it 'fore you don't need legs at all," Duffy said.

That gambler just looked up at Duffy. His eyes was pleadin' for mercy, but Duffy didn't have much of that left. Finally, Duffy relented a little and turned around and looked at some of them that was now in the saloon.

"You and you," he said as he pointed toward a couple of strong lookin' men. "Get him up and take him over to Doc's. Once he's got that leg looked after, see to it he's run out of town. While you're at it get them other two out of here."

That gambler and the wounded cowboy was taken over to Doc's. The cowboy weren't

223

hurt all that bad. He was patched up and escorted to the edge of town where he was advised not to return or thin's might not go too well for him.

The Doc, he fixed up that gambler as best he could, then went to talk to Duffy. He told Duffy that gambler weren't able to ride and wouldn't be fer a couple of days. Duffy gave in and told the Doc that the gambler had four days, and only four days to get out of town and never come back.

Everyone in town got to wonderin' if Duffy would keep his word. They was even takin' bets on what would happen if the gambler stayed past the four days.

Durin' them days, Duffy spent a lot of time in the saloon playin' cards. With him as Marshall, nothing much seemed to happen around town. On the fourth day, that gambler fella was put on a horse and escorted out of town.

That evenin' Duffy spent in the saloon playin' a bit of cards with some of the town folks, and I might add he took a bit of money off them. But in the mornin', Duffy was no where to be found. When I went over to the hotel room where he'd been stayin', it was empty, except for that Marshall's badge. It was on the dresser in his room.

Duffy McClue had come into town from nowhere, and disappeared just as quick. Some say he went up north, some say he went down south. I don't think anyone really knows where he went. One thin' for sure, no one ever laid eyes on him again.

THE TRAIN ROBBERY

It was a cold late September morning in the town of Deadwood in the Dakota Territory. A locomotive was next to the railroad station. Steam rolled off the boiler of the locomotive as a light drizzle continued to fall after last night's heavy rain. A light gray smoke slowly rolled out of the smokestack of the locomotive and drifted back over the train and off into the gray sky to disappear in the hazy mist.

The train was made up of four cars, a locomotive and a tender. One of the cars, a mail car, was located directly behind the locomotive's tender. There were two passenger cars behind the mail car and a caboose at the end. The train was waiting for the morning passengers and a shipment of gold from the Homestack Gold Mine.

The engineer and the fireman had stoked the locomotive and it was ready to go. The only thing holding up the train was the shipment of gold and the guards who were to protect it.

Those guarding the shipment were made up of four deputies from the Sheriff's Office in Deadwood and one Pinkerton agent by the name of Bart Thompson. Agent Thompson paced back and forth along the platform of the railroad station as he waited for the shipment of gold to arrive from the mine.

Agent Thompson was a tall slender man with dark brown wavy hair and deep brown eyes. His eyes were always moving as he took in everything that surrounded him. He wore a wide-brimmed hat that shaded his eyes. He also wore a long coat over his black suit and tall black riding boots. Under his long coat he carried two .45 caliber pistols in a cross-draw holster.

Agent Thompson was feared or respected, depending on which side of the law you were on. He had a reputation for bringing his prisoners in draped over a saddle. Very few who had tangled with him were alive to tell about it and he always said very little himself.

It was getting close to seven in the morning when a wagon with four men riding on it came around the corner to the railroad station. There were two men sitting on the wagon seat and two sitting on the rear of the wagon. As the wagon pulled up along side the railroad station, one of the guards jumped off the back of the wagon and ran up to Thompson.

"We're ready, sir," the guard said.

"Let's get it loaded," Thompson replied.

Before any of the guards moved, they waited for Thompson to take one more look around to make sure all was ready. When he was satisfied it was clear, he gave them the signal to start moving the gold from the wagon to the mail car on the train.

Once the signal was given, Thompson watched as one of the men sitting on the seat of the wagon tossed a double barrel shotgun down to one of the other guards then jumped down off the wagon. A deputy by the name of Willcut took up a position between the mail car and the wagon. Another deputy by the name of Swenson took a position several feet away from Willcut with his back toward him.

The other two deputies began loading the gold directly into the mail car where it was quickly secured in a large safe. With two of the deputies and Thompson standing guard, the loading of the shipment of gold went smoothly.

As soon as the gold was loaded and secured, one of the deputies climbed aboard the mail car then locked the door behind him. The other guard boarded the locomotive. Deputy Willcut boarded the train and took up his position at the end of the passenger car closest to the mail car. Deputy Swenson went to the back of the train and got aboard the caboose.

After all the deputies were in position, Agent Thompson stood on the platform and watched the passengers as they boarded the train. He took notice of all the passengers who boarded, especially those who boarded the passenger car closest to the mail car. There were seven passengers who boarded the car.

There were five men, a woman and one child about seven or eight years old. Thompson figured he could disregard one of the men and the woman, as they seemed to be the parents of the child. He had seen them together earlier on a bench on the station platform talking before they boarded.

One of the other men looked like he might be a traveling salesman. He wore a suit that was frayed at the cuffs and a coat that was in no better shape. The short, heavyset old man carried a carpetbag and a wooden box with the name of a company that made barbed wire on the side of it. He seemed to take little interest in the rest of the passengers. From the way he acted, he looked like he was used to traveling on the train.

Two of the remaining male passengers had caught Thompson's attention and caused him concern. The two were dressed like cowboys except for the fact they were well armed and carried their guns lower than most cowboys. The older one looked like someone Thompson should know, but he couldn't place where or when he had seen him, nor could he think of his name.

If it had been up the Thompson, he would have had them arrested, or at least removed from the train, but he had no reason to do either. He would have to keep a close eye on them and hope that they were not there for the gold.

The last man to board the train looked like a dude from back east somewhere. Thompson paid little attention to him as it was time to get the train moving.

With the gold loaded and everyone on board, there was nothing left for Thompson to do but give the conductor the signal to get the train rolling. Thompson motioned to the conductor who was standing on the platform near the rear of the second passenger car. He watched as the conductor signaled the engineer.

Black smoke belched out of the smokestack of the steam locomotive and the train lunged forward with a jerk. It started out very slowly gradually picking up speed.

Thompson took hold of the handrail of the first passenger car and swung up onto the car's step. As the train began to move away from the station, he looked around to see who might be watching the train as it left the station, but he didn't see anyone who held any interest for him.

As the train began to move faster, Thompson moved to the door of the passenger car and stepped inside. He took a seat on the left side of the car just to one side of the door. From there he could see where everyone in the passenger car was seated.

He could also see Deputy Willcut standing inside the door at the other end of the car. He was holding his shotgun loosely in his hands as he looked over the passengers. There was no question in Thompson's mind that Willcut was alert to his surroundings.

The train moved out of town and started into the narrow canyon that twisted its way toward Spearfish. The train moved slowly, winding its way like a snake through the canyon. The steady clicking of the iron wheels of the cars across the joints in the track and the sound of the steam engine chugging along filled the air with an almost musical rhythm.

Agent Thompson sat with his eyes roaming around the car. He watched as Deputy Willcut moved into the corner on the right side of the car with his back to the wall. From there he could see everyone in the car and most of what they were doing.

The young family caught Agent Thompson's attention and held it for a short time. They were sitting on the right side of the car almost in the middle. The little girl seemed excited as she looked out the window. She was so full of questions that she kept both her parents busy answering them. It was obvious this was the little girl's first ride on a train. Thompson could not help but smile as he thought back to his first train ride.

Agent Thompson looked over at the traveling salesman who had taken a seat on the left side of the car a couple of rows back from the young family. It was far from his first train ride. He had almost instantly tipped back, pulled his hat down over his eyes and went to sleep.

Thompson's eyes continued to roam around the car. One of the men that had boarded the train was seated directly across the aisle from him. Thompson didn't like having him there, but he had no indication he was anything other than a normal passenger. He appeared to be traveling alone and there was no logical reason for Thompson to ask him to sit somewhere else.

He had boarded the train well after the two men Thompson was suspicious of, and was seated at the opposite end of the car. He had not made any eye contact with the others, so Thompson had no reason to think they were together. He was dressed a good deal nicer than the other two. He wore a long coat and an eastern style hat. He also wore a pair of riding boots much like those seen back east. Thompson got the impression he might be a gambler who was more accustomed to being on a riverboat or in some gambling parlor located somewhere east of the Mississippi River than on a train.

Agent Thompson's attention turned to the other two men who were in the car. They had seated themselves on the left side of the car a few rows back from the front. Thompson could not get it out of his mind that he knew the older of the two men. It was unsettling for him to have seen the man's face as he boarded the train and not remember where he had seen him before. Right now the older man was sitting with his back to Thompson, but the young man was sitting across from him facing Thompson. The two were talking, but Thompson could not hear what they were saying.

Although the younger man tried to hide it, it was clear to Thompson that he was taking a bit more interest in him then he liked. It made Thompson wonder if the older man had told the younger one who he was. It was fast becoming clear to Thompson that if anything went wrong on this trip, it would come from those two.

Suddenly, there was the loud clanking of train couplers slamming together and the train began to slow down rather quickly. Thompson immediately knew what was about to happen and dove down below the back of the seat in front of him and drew his guns.

A shot was fired, then another. Thompson looked around the end of the seat in front of him and could see Deputy Willcut stagger slightly, then fall back against the corner of the car and slide down onto the floor.

"I wouldn't move if I were you," the man sitting across from Thompson said.

Thompson slowly turned his head and looked at the man. He had a short-barreled gun in his hand and it was pointed at him.

"Kindly drop the guns," the man said with a British accent.

Thompson reluctantly dropped his guns on the floor of the car.

The man slowly stood up, never taking his eyes off Thompson.

"Get up, old chap. I know this is a little embarrassing for you, but I'm sure you understand we couldn't take any unnecessary chances now, could we?"

"I'm sure," Thompson said as he slowly stood up.

Thompson looked at the man, then turned and looked toward the front of the car. He could see the two other men were standing. The older man had his gun pointed at the family, while the younger man was keeping watch on the salesman. The family all huddled together hoping no harm would come to them.

"Now, folks, I see no reason for anyone to get hurt. If you all do as you are told, this will be over in a few minutes and you can continue on your journey."

"Who are you?" Thompson asked.

"I don't think that is important, but since you asked, the name is James Holden. I won't ask you to embarrass yourself, as I already know who you are. You are the famous Pinkerton agent Bert Thompson."

"Sorry, but you got that wrong. I'm Bart Thompson."

"Sorry old chap, but it really isn't going to matter who you are. You see, we are going to take the gold off this train and then disappear. You will never find us."

"I wouldn't count on that," Thompson replied.

"But I am counting on that," Holden said with a grin.

"Let's get at it. We don't have all day," the older man said.

"Relax," Holden replied. "We are in the middle of nowhere. Who's going to bother us here?"

"No one, I guess," the older man said.

The sound of his voice caused Thompson to remember who the older man was. It was Bill Whitman, a two-bit robber who had apparently moved up to robbing trains.

"Say, Bill, didn't you explain to your British friend here that it won't be easy to get into the mail car?"

"We've got a way in," Bill replied with a grin.

"Then I suggest we get started, gentlemen," Holden said.

"Sure. Kid, you keep an eye on these good folks. We don't want nothing to happen to them while we're openin' up the mail car."

Holden motioned for Thompson to move to the front of the car. Thompson knew he had little choice in the matter. He would have to do what he was told, at least until his chance came.

Thompson was pushed into the seat where Bill had been sitting. He sat down and looked up at Holden.

"Keep a close eye on this one. He will be the only one here to give you any trouble," Holden told the kid.

Thompson watched as Holden and Bill moved to the front of the car and stepped out the door onto the steps. Holden put his gun in his holster under his coat and then got off the train.

"What's going on?" Holden called out as he stepped out into the open where the guard on the engine could see him.

By stepping out in the open, it made it appear as if there was nothing wrong on the train. The guard should have known something was wrong, as it was not Thompson who had stepped off the train. He leaned out of the side of the engine and looked toward Holden.

"There's a tree across the tracks," the engineer called back.

While the guard was looking out at Holden, Bill ran down the other side of the train. He came up behind the guard and shot him in the back.

The fireman and the engineer also had their backs to Bill and had not seen him come up behind them. They quickly ducked down at the sound of gunfire and hoped Bill would not shoot them, too.

"You two stay right where you are," Bill said as he pointed his gun first at one then the other.

Thompson watched the kid very closely. He noticed that although the kid had his gun pointed at him, he was always looking around. There was little doubt in his mind the kid was nervous. He came to the conclusion it might be the kid's first holdup. If it was, there was no telling what he might do being as he was so nervous.

"They're going to leave you as soon as they get the gold," Thompson said softly.

The kid stared at him for a moment or two, trying to decide if what he said might be true.

"They wouldn't do that to me," the kid insisted. "We're partners."

"Why wouldn't they?"

Just then, there was the sound of an explosion. Thompson instantly knew Bill and Holden had used dynamite to blow open the mail car door.

The sudden noise caused the kid to turn his attention for just a second to what was going on outside. It was all Thompson needed. He took the opportunity.

Just as the kid was turning back around, Thompson lunged at him. He caught the kid on the chin with his hard right hand as he dove for the kid's gun. The two of them went crashing to the floor. While keeping hold of the gun in the kid's hand so he could not shoot it, Thompson hit the kid again and again until the kid let go of the gun and could no longer put up a fight.

Thompson got up and looked down at the kid on the floor for just a second. The kid was out cold. He then grabbed up the shotgun that had been carried by Willcut, turned and looked at the man who was huddled with his family.

"You know how to use this?" he demanded.

"Yes," the man replied as he stood up.

"Keep an eye on this one. Stay in the car," Thompson said as he tossed the shotgun to the man.

Suddenly there were several gunshots from outside the train. It was clear to Thompson that the guard in the mail car was putting up a fight. There was no time to waste. He would need help and he would need it now.

Thompson quickly turned and ran to the back of the car. He carefully stepped out of the car. He leaned down and looked around the corner toward the mail car.

Just as he looked around the corner of the car, Bill caught a glimpse of him. He fired off a shot that hit the corner of the passenger car.

Thompson ducked back around the corner. He was confused by what he saw.

Bill was standing close to the mail car, but away from the door. It appeared that the guard in the car had given him reason to stay back.

The air was suddenly filled with gunfire. Shots were coming from the rocks off to the side along the canyon wall. Shots were being returned from the rear of the train and some from the mail car. A bullet slammed into the passenger car just above Thompson's head. The train had been stopped here as part of an ambush. The rest of the gang had been waiting for them just in case there was trouble.

Thompson quickly joined in with the other law officers in putting up a fight. Glass from the windows of the passenger car was flying around, bullets shattered pieces of trim and seat cushions were being ripped apart by bullets.

Thompson returned fire with deadly accuracy. One of his bullets struck the man in the rocks that had been shooting at him. Thompson didn't have time to watch as another of the outlaws fell from the rocks and landed in the stream that ran close to the tracks, he was too busy.

Suddenly, he felt a sharp pain in his left arm. He quickly ducked back inside the car. A look at his left arm showed he had been hit, but it didn't look serious. He quickly wrapped his arm with a handkerchief and got back into the fight.

Gradually the shooting seemed to slow. There were still a few shots coming from toward the rear of the train and in the middle, but there were no more shots coming from near the mail car.

Thompson slowly looked out around the corner of the passenger car. He caught a glimpse of Holden and Bill taking off on horseback. He fired a couple of shots at them. He saw Bill fall off his horse just as Holden turned and disappeared around some rocks.

Without thinking, Thompson jumped down off the train and ran toward where he had shot Bill. He was not thinking about what was ahead of him, he was interested in one thing. He was not going to let Holden escape with the gold he had been assigned to protect.

It took him a couple of very valuable minutes to get hold of Bill's horse. When he got to it, the horse was a little skittish and was hard for him to catch. Each minute was wasting valuable time.

He was finally able to grab the reins of the horse and get mounted. Thompson kicked the horse in the ribs and was quickly in pursuit of Holden. He knew he was far behind, but Holden was leaving a trail in the soft wet dirt. As Thompson pushed on, he gave thanks for the rain last night. As long as Holden stayed on the trail, he would be able to follow him.

Thompson came to a split in the trail and reined up. It was easy to see which way Holden had gone, but if Thompson remembered correctly, the trail to the left would take him to the same place. More importantly, it was shorter.

Thompson quickly decided he would take the chance and take the shortcut. It might save him enough time to at least get closer to Holden. Anything that might cut the distance between them he would do.

Thompson kicked the horse in the sides and raced down the narrow trail. It was partially overgrown and the small thin branches of the overhanging trees slapped at him like lashes from a whip.

When the two trails came together again, Thompson saw the tracks of Holden's horse in the mud. He didn't know how much, if any, he had gained on him. He was at least feeling better about his decision to take the other trail. It wasn't until he came around a bend in the trail with a fairly long straight section that he caught a glimpse of Holden.

Holden saw him almost immediately. He turned in the saddle and fired a shot at Thompson, but it went wild. Holden tried to push his horse on; but with the extra weight of two saddlebags of gold, his horse was beginning to tire.

It soon became clear to Holden that he could not outrun Thompson. He would have to find a place to stop and fight. It was only a short distance before Holden saw a place that looked like a good place to put up a fight.

He reined up, grabbed the saddlebags off the horse and dove into the rocks. By the time he had gotten behind the rocks and could look back down the trail, there was no one in sight.

Thompson had suddenly disappeared. There was no sign of him or the horse.

Holden became very nervous. He was out of his element here in the rocky outcroppings and thick woods of the Black Hills. He was used to gambling halls and saloons where the only places to hide were behind bars or tables. He knew he was quick with a gun, and at short distances he could hit what he wanted. Out here in the open there were so many places to hide behind it was hard to watch them all. Accuracy at greater distances was far more important than quickness.

Holden began to sweat. It was beginning to cross his mind that the robbery of the train might not have been planned out as well as he thought. He had not counted on anyone being so dedicated and determined to capture him.

"You ready to give it up," Thompson called out.

Holden slowly stuck his head up over the outcropping of rock he had hidden behind and looked around. He was not sure where the voice was coming from. Down in the canyon among the rocky cliffs, the jagged outcroppings and the thick trees, it was hard to determine where the sound was coming from.

Suddenly a shot was fired and the bullet smashed into the rocky outcropping not more than a few inches from Holden's head. He quickly ducked back down. He had not seen where the shot had come from. It was becoming clear to him that Thompson could probably take him out anytime he was ready.

Holden had heard of Thompson. He knew Thompson's reputation for bringing back outlaws slung over a saddle. He was beginning to think seriously about giving up. The only thing that prevented him from surrendering was the sheer fact he knew either way he was a dead man. If Thompson didn't kill him, he would certainly hang for his part in the killing of the guards on the train. His only chance was to fight it out with Thompson.

"I guess you are going to have to come and get me," Holden said, his voice showing he had resigned himself to what might come of it.

"We don't have to play it out this way," Thompson called back.

"Yes, we do. This is between you and me now. Only one of us will walk away from this."

There was a long period of silence. It seemed the longer it went on the more nervous Holden became. The palms of his hands were so sweaty he could hardly hold onto his pistol. The sweat ran down his face even though the day was cold and looked like it might snow at any time.

Suddenly there was the sound of a single gunshot, the slug hitting high above Holden's head. It caused several small pieces of rock to shower down on him, causing him to almost panic.

"You can't stay there forever," Thompson called out.

Holden quickly ran across a small open area into another group of rocks. He was not sure if he would be any safer there, but it had become clear that he was not safe where he had been. As he ducked down, another shot was fired and rocks again showered down on him.

"Not a good place to hide."

The tension in Holden's body was building rapidly. He could not see where Thompson was hiding. He had nothing to shoot at that would have any affect on his situation. Holden was beginning to feel it was hopeless, that he would not win this fight no matter what he did.

Once again he tried to move to a place he felt might provide him with some protection and make it harder for Thompson to find him. Once again it proved futile. A single shot rang out and it hit close to him again. It was beginning to look as if there was no place he could go that Thompson could not get at him. He was feeling a sense of futility wash over him. There was nothing he could do except to give up.

With no escape in sight, he began to think about what would happen to him. The only possible chance he could see to live would be to give up. He reasoned that at least if he gave up, he might find an opportunity to escape from jail while he waited to be hung. It was not much of a choice, but it was better than dying in among the rocks.

"You win," Holden called out. "I give up."

"Come out onto the trail where I can see you. And come out with your hands up," Thompson instructed him.

Holden did as he was told. He stood up and worked his way out of the rocks back to the trail. When he got to the trail, he dropped his gun on the ground and raised his hands above his head.

Once Holden was standing on the trail, Thompson came out from the cover of the rocks and trees. He walked up to Holden with his gun pointed at him.

"Turn around and start walking."

It wasn't long before they came to the horse Thompson had been riding in the chase. On the saddle was a rope. Thompson tied Holden to a tree then went after the other horse.

Once Thompson had both horses and had retrieved the saddlebags of gold, he took his prisoner back to where the train was still stopped. He could see the bodies of six men neatly laid out along side the tracks. The outlaws had lost four men and he had lost two of his guards. Six men in all had died in the attempt to rob the train of its gold. Thompson had to wonder if it was all worth it.

Thompson looked up and saw Swenson walking toward him. He had his gun in his hand and had a smile on his face.

"Looks like you got your man. I see you've been hit. How are you doing?" Swenson asked as he stood in front of Thompson.

"I'm okay. Just a scratch. Did we get them all?" Thompson asked as he looked around.

"Yup."

"I think it would be a good idea if we got this train moving again," Thompson suggested. "Let's get the bodies on the train."

Once all the bodies had been put on the train and his prisoners were secured in shackles, Thompson sat down and leaned back. The steady clicking of the iron wheels on the track was a peaceful sound to him. He had his man, the gold was safe and, all in all, everything was as it should be.

THE CHEYENNE RIVER INCIDENT

Captain Ben Wheeler was being transferred and had been reassigned as the new commander of a U.S. Army outpost in northwestern Nebraska not very far south of the Black Hills. He was to take command of a company of soldiers whose job it was to provide protection for the white settlers who were traveling through the area on their way west.

Captain Wheeler had been stationed in northern Virginia and had no experience with Indians. On his way to his new assignment, he was to make stops at a fort in Minnesota and then on to Fort Pierre in the Dakota Territory with supplies. From there he was to travel alone to his new assignment in Nebraska. Although he had been told numerous stories about the savages that lived out west, he really knew nothing about the red man. It should suffice to say he had little or no knowledge of what was referred to as the Frontier.

Captain Wheeler had been traveling alone for a number of weeks when he came to the Cheyenne River. He planned to follow the river until he came to the southern end of the Black Hills where he would find a stream he could follow that would lead him to the fort, at least that is what he had been told.

During his travels across the open prairie he had not seen a single Indian, nor had he seen any of the large herds of buffalo he had been told roamed the plains. All he had seen were a few mule deer and a couple of herds of antelope. So far he had not had any problems, but that was to change soon.

It was late one evening when he had made his camp along the south bank of the Cheyenne River. He had arrived at his present campsite just before dark and decided it might be best to set up a dry camp tonight, one without a fire. He had not seen anything to indicate he should be cautious, but he felt it was a good idea just to be on the safe side.

After he had eaten his ration of hard tack and jerky, he rolled out his bedroll under the cottonwood trees in the hope of getting a good night's sleep. Lying under his covers he could hear the sounds of an owl in a tree a little way down the river. There was the mournful cry of a coyote off in the distance as well. He listened to the sounds of the night for awhile before he fell into a deep sleep.

For some unknown reason, Captain Wheeler had slept late. He was used to getting up before daylight, but this morning the sun was up and already starting to warm the cool morning air when he opened his eyes. He stretched and tried to get the stiffness out of his muscles from sleeping on the cool damp ground. As he sat up, he thought he could hear voices. They seemed to be coming from the other side of the river.

Being as quiet as he could, he crawled out of his bedroll and rolled over near a fallen cottonwood tree that lay between him and the river. He picked up his gun and slowly rose up to peer over the top of the log.

The sight of several Indian women washing clothes in the river startled him. He quickly ducked back down and took a deep breath. Where there were Indian women, there were bound to be braves watching over them. His mind filled with questions of what he should do.

He rose up again so he could see over the log. As he looked around, he discovered two young braves keeping watch over the women. One of the braves was sitting on his horse, half hidden among the trees near the bank of the river. The brave had a long lance with feathers dangling from it in his hand as he looked up and down the river. Captain Wheeler watched the brave as he nudged his horse out of the trees and into ankle deep water.

There was another brave sitting on a horse at the edge of the river. He was also keeping a sharp lookout. The two braves did not seem to be paying any attention to the women as they chatted away while they washed clothes.

As Captain Wheeler watched the Indian women, he began to wonder where their camp might be. He had not seen any signs of a camp, yet there were four or five women at the edge of the river. There had to be more Indians close by.

Captain Wheeler began looking around in an effort to find out where the Indians' camp might be. When he looked up above the trees on the other side of the river, he could see just a hint of smoke drifting lazily above the trees. The Indians had a camp back away from the river. Since there was smoke coming from the camp, it was apparent that they were not expecting any trouble.

He again looked down at the river. Although he could see only two braves, he was sure if one of the braves were to see him and send up an alarm, there would be more braves coming to their aid in a matter of minutes.

Captain Wheeler turned around and sat down with his back against the log. He looked at his campsite and at his horses that were tied maybe twenty feet or so away. He realized it was something of a miracle that the Indians had not seen them already. They seemed to him to be standing almost out in the opening, as the trees were so sparse. The horses were paying no attention to what was going on. They continued to eat the thick green grass that grew among the trees.

Captain Wheeler was trying to figure out how he was going to get away from here without being seen by the two warriors. He knew the river was shallow and easy to cross here. It would take them no time at all to get across the river to him. They could probably get to him before he could get to his horses.

He began to think that if he ran to his horses and left everything he had behind, he might be able to get away. On the other hand, if he stayed out of sight and didn't do anything to make a sound, he might be able to wait them out.

How long can it take those women to wash their clothes, he wondered? It certainly couldn't take them very long. On the other hand, how long would it be before they saw his horses and came after them?

He ducked back down, then rolled over on his stomach and crawled to the end of the log. Lying flat, he peered around the end of the log. He noticed one of the Indian women was a rather nice looking young woman. She smiled and laughed with the women, but seemed not to join in as much as the others. Captain Wheeler became fascinated with her and watched her as she worked.

The young Indian woman had skin tanned by the sun giving it a glow in the morning sun. Her hair was a dark brown and was pulled back and braided, and sparkled like sunlight on the water. Her long skirt was pulled up and tucked into her beaded belt showing off her legs as she waded in the water to rinse a piece of clothing.

It was at that moment Captain Wheeler realized the young woman's legs were far too light in color for her to be an Indian, and the color of her hair did not seem dark enough, either. The more he watched her, the more he became aware of the woman's features, and they were those of a white woman.

He had heard about Indians taking white women as prisoners then taking them into the tribe. He had to wonder if this was the case with this woman.

The woman looked up at one of the braves as he nudged his horse beside her. She smiled up at him and said something, but Captain Wheeler could not hear what she said. He did notice the brave smiled back at her. It made him wonder if she might be his woman.

That thought quickly brought Captain Wheeler back to his situation. Should he stay and hope they didn't see him or his horses, or should he try to make a run for it? The question was soon to be decided for him.

The other brave who had been sitting astride his horse on the bank of the river turned and looked toward where Captain Wheeler was hiding. He had simply been looking around when he spotted the captain's horses standing in among the trees. Captain Wheeler heard the warrior yell something and point toward the horses.

In a flash, the two braves were charging across the river while the women were grabbing up their things and running back into the brush along the river's edge, all except for the white woman. She stood up and looked off across the river.

Captain Wheeler readied himself to defend his little camp, but quickly realized it would be a useless effort. He might be able to stop the attack by the two braves, but he would surely be set upon by many more braves before he could escape.

The yell by one of the braves had quickly brought out several other Indians from the trees that lined the north side of the river. Now there were a dozen or more braves charging across the river, some on foot while others were on horseback.

Captain Wheeler remembered that he had heard somewhere that Indians respected brave men. He knew he could not win a fight against all of them. He felt his best chance was to stand up straight, look them right in the eye and hope they didn't kill him.

He stood up, placed his gun on the log and then stood tall as he watched the warriors ride at full clip across the river. He could not help but notice the braves as they closed in on him. They were strong and fearless in their appearance and manner. Their skin was a reddish brown in color and their faces showed their determination to defend their camp.

As the first of the braves came close, Captain Wheeler raised his hand in a sign of peace. He had no idea what the young braves would do, but he hoped they would at least spare his life. He had no hatred for them, but was not sure how they felt about him, a white man on their land.

The first brave to get close to him threw his lance. He did not intend to kill the captain with it as it stuck in the ground several inches in front of him. Captain Wheeler stood his ground and continued to hold his hand up. Although he was scared to death of what they might do, he hoped his passive approach would be thought of as a sign of peace, not of weakness.

It was the second brave that struck the first blow. As Captain Wheeler stood tall with his hand up, the second brave rode very close to him. As he charged past him, the brave's foot shot out and kicked him, sending Captain Wheeler sprawling on his back after spinning around.

As he rolled over and got up on his hands and knees to stand up, another brave rode by him and swung his club at Captain Wheeler's head. The club struck a glancing blow along side the captain's head and rolled him over on his back again. The blow to his head had dazed him, but he did not lose consciousness.

Everything was hazy, nothing seemed real to him.

Before he knew what was happening, there were several braves around him. With his senses dazed, he could comprehend only bits and pieces of what was happening to him. He could feel his hands were being tied with rawhide strips and then he was pulled to his feet. He could feel a rope being slipped over his head and around his neck.

There was a sudden jerk of the rope as one of the Indians started pulling him toward the river. Captain Wheeler stumbled, as he was led into the river. As the fog cleared from his head it came to him that they were taking him to their camp.

Stumbling along, he got a glimpse of the white woman. Although it was just a glimpse of her, he thought he could see a concerned look in her eyes. He tried to say something to her, but the brave who had the end of the rope gave a sharp tug on it sending the captain splashing into the river.

The Indian dragged him almost to the north bank of the river before stopping to look over his shoulder. He was laughing while the captain tried to get to his feet. When he finally got to his feet, the brave once again moved on toward the village.

As the captain was led into the village, he got his first look at it. It was a small village with only a couple of dozen teepees. There were only a few children, several women and a number of warriors ranging in age from young adults to old men. It was one of the old men that caught the captain's attention.

"Where did you find this man?" the elderly warrior asked in his native language.

"He was spying on us from across the river," the young brave replied.

The young brave went on to explain how they had captured him. Although Captain Wheeler could not understand what was being said, it was clear by the gestures the brave made while telling his story that he was most likely talking about him. It also struck Captain Wheeler as a bit funny that it was taking so long for this brave to tell his story. He was sure he was doing a little bragging, too.

"Is there anyone here who can speak English," Captain Wheeler asked as he stood soaking wet while looking at the elderly warrior.

Everything stopped. All the Indians who had gathered around to see this man looked at him as if he had broken some sacred rule. No one said a word, they just looked at him and each other as if wondering what he was saying.

Finally, the white woman he had seen at the river stepped out from behind a couple of other women. She walked over next to the elderly warrior and stood silently looking at the ground. It came to the captain's mind this elderly warrior must be the chief.

"Will you speak to him for us?" the chief asked.

"If you wish," she replied in their native tongue.

"Ask him why he is here?"

The woman spoke very slowly in fairly good English. She asked the question the chief told her to ask and said nothing more.

"Is he your chief?' Captain Wheeler asked instead of answering her question.

"Yes. He is Chief Gray Wolf," she replied.

"Tell your chief I'm on my way to Fort Robinson, and I wish no harm to him or his people."

The woman told the chief what he had said.

"Ask him his reason for being this far north of the fort."

The white woman did as she was told.

"Tell him that I went up the Missouri River to Fort Pierre to deliver supplies then to Cheyenne River. From there I came to the foot of the Black Hills where I was going to turn south to the fort."

"But that is the long way," the woman said.

"Maybe so, but it is the only way I know," he replied.

"What is he saying," Gray Wolf asked.

The white woman turned to Gray Wolf and took a moment to tell the chief what had been said. She explained that she didn't think he was there to spy on them. He was just lost and was trying to find the fort.

The chief looked at the woman, then turned and looked at the captain. He was suspicious of the white man in a soldier's uniform with good reason. He had learned many years ago not to trust the white man.

"Tie him to that tree," Gray Wolf said, pointing to a large Ponderosa pine. "We will meet to talk about him."

With that said, the captain was taken to the tree where he was tied. Although the braves had handled him roughly, he did not complain or make a sound. After he was tied, two young braves stood nearby to guard him.

Captain Wheeler watched what was going on. Several of the older warriors had gathered around a fire with the chief to talk. He was sure they were all members of the tribe's council. There was no doubt in his mind they were there to decide his fate.

Those gathered around the fire talked about what they should do with their prisoner. Some of the younger members of the council were in favor of killing him, but the older members were not in such a hurry to do him harm.

"This is but one lost soldier. He can do us no harm," White Horse said, a member of the council who was a little younger than Gray Wolf.

"What do you say, Running Elk?" Gray Wolf asked.

"If we do not kill him, he will tell the horse soldiers where we are and that there is a white woman in our camp. Many horse soldiers will come and attack our village. To let him go would bring death to us all," Running Elk said, the youngest member of the council.

"You have a point, but should we kill him and the horse soldiers find out, they will come and kill us anyway," Red Eagle said.

Several of the council members began to argue back and forth. Emotions were running very high. They were in disagreement as to what to do with their prisoner.

"Enough, enough," Gray Wolf called out in an effort to stop the arguing. "We need time to think. We need to know what kind of a man this horse soldier is."

"And how do we find that out?" Running Elk asked.

"We have Little Dove talk to him. She will help us find out what kind of a man he is."

"But she is white. She will side with him," White Horse protested.

"She is one of us," Gray Wolf insisted. "She has been with us for many moons now. She has proven she can be trusted. She will find out what is in his heart. She will do this for us."

There was a great deal of mumbling among the council members, but they all knew Gray Wolf's word was law. He made the final decision. To argue with him once he had decided what was to be done would weaken that member's standing with the others.

"We will meet back here when the sun is high in the sky," Gray Wolf said.

Each of the council members stood up and left the area. Gray Wolf sat next to the fire and stared into it. He was not sure what he should do. He had lived a long time and had been in many battles both with the whites and with other Indian tribes. He had seen the results of those battles. There had been many lodges where the women and children had wept for their lost braves. He wanted to see no more blood shed upon the land.

Gray Wolf finally looked up and began looking around as if he was looking for someone. When he saw Little Dove, he called to her.

"Little Dove, I must talk to you."

Little Dove looked a bit surprised that Gray Wolf had called for her, but she had a pretty good idea what he wanted. She quickly walked over to the fire and stood silently close to him and waited for him to speak first.

"Little Dove, I want you to go to the horse soldier and talk to him. I want you to find out what is in his heart."

"I can't," she said as she looked down at the ground.

"You can. He is of your kind."

"But I am no longer his kind," she protested.

"You are, and you will know if what he says is true. You need to talk to him for us."

Little Dove looked at the old man's face. He wanted her to do this for the tribe. He would not have asked her if it wasn't important. Reluctantly, she nodded that she would talk to the horse soldier.

Gray Wolf watched her as she walked toward where Captain Wheeler was tied. Little Dove's steps slowed as she approached him. She was even a little scared of him, yet there was something about him that intrigued her.

Captain Wheeler's head ached from the hit on his head and he was cold from being wet. The ropes on his hands and feet were extremely uncomfortable, but he was still alive. He was unsure of how long that would last, but his hope for survival improved when he saw Little Dove coming toward him.

Little Dove walked up in front of the captain and stood there looking down at him. She glanced over at the two braves standing guard over him. It made her feel a little better knowing that the braves were close by and the horse soldier was securely tied.

"Gray Wolf, our chief, wants to know what is in your heart?" she asked.

"I don't understand," he replied, a confused look on his face.

"Why are you here?"

"I told you, I'm on my way to Fort Robinson."

"You are very far north of there. This is the long way to the white man's fort."

"So you tell me."

"What were you doing on the other side of the river?" she asked.

"I was camping there."

"Without a fire?"

"I thought it best not to have one."

"Then you were watching us."

"No, well, yes. I was watching you wash clothes this morning. But when I came to this place last night, I didn't know you and the others were here."

"Why didn't you run?"

"I didn't think it was wise to run. I meant no harm to any of you."

Little Dove looked into his eyes as he spoke to her. There was something about the way he looked and the words he spoke that made her want to believe him. But there was also the fact he was a horse soldier. The people of her tribe had told her that if the horse soldiers ever found out a white woman was in their tribe, they would stop at nothing to take her away.

"Did you come to take me away?" she asked.

"No. I didn't know you were here. Do you want to leave here?" Captain Wheeler asked.

"No. I am happy here," she replied.

"But you are a white woman. Wouldn't you like to be with other white women?"

"No. I have my friends here."

Little Dove could hardly remember any of the white people she had known. The tribe had taken her in when she was only ten or eleven. They had found her as the only survivor of a raid on a wagon train made by another tribe. They had taken care of her, and Gray Wolf and his wife had raised her as one of their own. She had no family other than Gray Wolf's family.

Little Dove found herself explaining how she had come to be with this small tribe of Indians. For some reason she found it easy to talk to him. There was something in his eyes that made her want to trust this man. She found him handsome even though he was soaking wet and he had streaks of blood down the side of his head from where he had been hit.

"They have been good to me. I would not want any harm to come to them," she said.

"They have been good to you so I do not wish any harm to come to them, either. How can I convince your chief and the others I wish them no harm?"

Little Dove looked into his eyes again as he spoke to her. In her heart, she was convinced he meant what he said, but she still had a twinge of doubt.

"Maybe I can arrange for you to talk to the council," she suggested.

"I would be grateful if you can do that."

"I will talk to them."

"Would it be possible for me to get cleaned up? I have dry clothes in my belongings."

Little Dove looked around before she spoke. "I will arrange it."

Little Dove turned and walked away. As she walked back toward Gray Wolf's teepee, she turned her head and glanced back at Captain Wheeler. He fascinated her. He seemed different from the few other white men the tribe would occasionally come in contact with. Most of them were hunters and traders.

Little Dove arranged for Captain Wheeler to get cleaned up. He was taken to a teepee where he was allowed to wash up, comb his hair and change into a clean dry uniform. He did the best he could to look like an officer with what little they gave him.

When he came out of the teepee, he stood up straight and tall. He wanted his captors to know he was not afraid of them, even if he was. He found himself quickly surrounded by several braves and led over to a teepee that had many drawings on it. There was also a fire out in front.

Sitting in front of the teepee was Chief Gray Wolf. He was dressed in deerskins that were decorated with colorful beads. He wore a headdress with many feathers in it. This was going to be a formal meeting, one that would probably decide Captain Wheeler's fate.

As Captain Wheeler came closer to the fire, he looked at the others sitting around it. They were all dressed in their finest. It gave him the feeling this was their court, and it was at this court he would have to defend himself.

For some strange reason it gave him a small degree of relief to see Little Dove seated beside Gray Wolf. He knew why she was there. She was to interpret for him and the others.

She was dressed in a deerskin dress with beadwork around the neck and down the sleeves. Even her boots were made of deerskin. He found it hard to take his eyes off her.

Gray Wolf looked up as Captain Wheeler stopped in front of the teepee. He motioned for Captain Wheeler to sit down in the only place left around the fire. Once Captain Wheeler was seated, Gray Wolf looked into the fire. It was almost as if he was saying a small prayer before things got started.

"I am Chief Gray Wolf of the Cheyenne Sioux tribe," he said.

Little Dove translated what all those sitting around the fire were saying.

"I am Captain Wheeler of the United States Army."

"Why have you come here?" Chief Gray Wolf asked.

"I am on my way to Fort Robinson. This is the way I was told to come."

"But it is the long way."

"So I have been told. I did not intend to disturb you and your people. I was simply spending the night across the river. I had planned to continue my trip this morning."

"It has become difficult for us to let you continue."

"Why is that? I have done nothing to you, and you have not done anything to me that I would hold against you."

"You have seen Little Dove," Gray Wolf replied.

"I don't understand?" Captain Wheeler said as he glanced at Little Dove.

"You will tell others of the white woman in our camp. Many horse soldiers will come and attack our camp and take her away," Running Elk said.

"You see why it is difficult for us to let you go?" Gray Wolf asked.

Captain Wheeler looked at Little Dove then back at Gray Wolf. He was beginning to understand what this was really all about. He had heard of attacks made on Indian villages because there had been reports of a white woman in the village; but if he remembered correctly, they were made because the white woman had been taken unwillingly. This was not the case here. If they had not taken Little Dove into their tribe, she would have most likely died alone on the prairie.

"I understand. You are afraid I will tell my people about Little Dove."

"That is right," Gray Wolf said.

"Little Dove told me how she came to be with you. Little Dove seems happy here. If it is her wish to stay here with you, then I can see no reason for me to tell anyone she is here."

"I don't believe we can trust him," White Horse said. "We have been lied to by other horse soldiers before. What makes this one any different?"

"I think that we should kill him and hide his body so the horse soldiers will never know he was here. That is the only way to be sure he will not tell," Running Elk said.

Captain Wheeler looked at Running Elk. He was a strong young brave and he did speak his heart. It was apparent Running Elk had his reasons not to trust the horse soldiers.

Captain Wheeler glanced over at Little Dove. She was looking at him. The expression on her face indicated to the captain she did not like the talk of killing him.

"The horse soldiers will know that something has happened to this man if he does not arrive at the fort. They will come looking for him, and when they don't find him they will find us. They will see Little Dove. We will not be able to hide her forever," Gray Wolf said sadly. "The spirits have shined on us for a long time and kept Little Dove out of the eyes of the horse soldiers."

Captain Wheeler could understand the dilemma Gray Wolf had been put in by his being there. Chief Gray Wolf was right. It was only a matter of time before a missionary, or a trader, or someone else saw her and told about her being in the tribe.

"I must have time to think," Gray Wolf said. "It is time to look to our future. Take the horse soldier to a teepee and guard him. We will meet here again later."

Little Dove walked with Captain Wheeler back to the teepee.

She went inside with him while two braves stood guard outside.

For the next few hours Little Dove asked him what life was like for a white woman in the white man's world. Captain Wheeler tried to be as honest as he could with her. He told her about the life of a white woman on the plains rather than the life of a woman in the eastern cities. He felt it would be easier for her to understand and believe.

After they had talked, Little Dove decided she needed some time to be alone. She had heard all that had been said around the council fire and all of what Captain Wheeler had said. It became clear to her that it was not Captain Wheeler who was putting her tribe in danger; it was her by just being there. She needed time to think, time to decide what she must do.

Little Dove went down by the river and sat on a rock. As she looked off across the river, she thought about what life would be like for her as a white woman in the white man's world. She could still remember a little about her mother and father, but her memory of them and what life had been like was growing dim.

Her thoughts turned to Captain Wheeler. She liked him and he had been nice to her. He was handsome and appeared to be smart. More importantly, he seemed to like her. She was convinced that he would keep his word. That thought set in motion a plan she hoped would make everything work out for the best for all.

Little Dove returned to the tent where Captain Wheeler was being held. She went inside and sat down with him. Looking at him, she hesitated for a minute before she told him what was on her mind.

"I've been thinking. If I go to Fort Robinson with you, the horse soldiers will not have any reason to attack my people. Will they?" she asked.

"No, they won't."

"My people will be safe?"

"I can't speak for anyone else, but I can assure you that your people will not have any problems with my troops."

"What will happen to me if I go to Fort Robinson with you?"

"That depends on you. If you want to find any of your relatives that may be alive, I will help you do that. If you want to stay at the fort, I will look after you.

"Do you like me?" Little Dove asked.

"Yes," he replied. "I like you."

"You will take care of me if I come to the fort with you?"

"Yes, if that is what you wish," he replied.

"Will I live with you as your wife?"

Captain Wheeler hadn't thought of it in that way, but surprisingly he didn't find any reason to object to it. He looked at her for a minute before he responded.

"If you want."

"You would do that for me and my people?"

"Yes," he replied.

"Then we need to talk to Gray Wolf. We need to make the arrangements soon so we can leave before the horse soldiers come looking for you."

Little Dove took Captain Wheeler by the hand and almost dragged him out of the teepee. They quickly found Gray Wolf and gathered the council together. After explaining their plan, all seemed to agree, although Running Elk had some reservation about Captain Wheeler.

Late that afternoon, Captain Wheeler and Little Dove were married by Gray Wolf. After a celebration and much feasting that lasted well into the night, they were directed to the same teepee he had been held captive in, but this time was different. For one thing there were no guards outside.

Once inside the teepee, the newlyweds got ready for bed. They were both a little nervous, but there seemed to be something between them that they could build a loving relationship on.

As Little Dove laid down and curled up beside Captain Wheeler under the buffalo blanket, she looked up at his face. She was happy at this moment even if a little unsure of her future.

"What was your name before you were called Little Dove."

"I was called Becky Tilman. I have not used that name for many years."

"From now on you will be Mrs. Ben Wheeler."

"I will not be called Little Dove any more?"

"Not by others. You will be called Becky Wheeler or Mrs. Ben Wheeler. But when we are alone, I will call you Little Dove if you wish."

"Ben Wheeler," she said thoughtfully. "That is a good name. I like it."

When morning came, Captain and Mrs. Wheeler were given a couple of rather plain horses that did not look too much like Indian ponies. One for Little Dove to ride and one to carry the gifts they had received. Captain Wheeler was given back his horses and supplies. Little Dove bid goodbye to her friends and family, then rode off with Captain Wheeler as his wife.

As the new post commander at Fort Robinson, Captain Wheeler didn't feel he would have any trouble with any of the other officers or the enlisted men. Little Dove would be accepted as his wife, Mrs. Ben Wheeler, without question.

www.ingramcontent.com/pod-product-compliance
Lightning Source LLC
Chambersburg PA
CBHW071120170626
46809CB00002B/438